STILL THE SAME MAN

JON BILBAO

Translated from the Spanish by
Sophie Hughes

HB Hispabooks
Publishing

Hispabooks Publishing, S. L.
Madrid, Spain
www.hispabooks.com

Originally published in Spain as *Padres, hijos y primates* by Salto de
    Página, 2011
First published in English by Hispabooks, 2016
English translation copyright © by Sophie Hughes
Design © simonpates - www.patesy.com

ISBN 978-84-943658-3-6 (trade paperback)
ISBN 978-84-943658-4-3 (ebook)
Legal Deposit: M-30629-2015

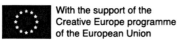

With the support of the
Creative Europe programme
of the European Union

The European Commission support for the production of this publication does not constitute an endorsement of the contents which reflects the views only of the authors, and the Commission cannot be held responsible for any use which may be made of the information contained therein.

A man doesn't alter because you find out more about him. He's still the same man.

GRAHAM GREENE, *The Third Man*

CONTENTS

PART I

Road

The animals were hiding, or perhaps they sensed what was coming and had fled inland looking for refuge. Since arriving in Mexico, Joanes had only seen birds—raucous and all pervasive—and the large-footed geckos that loitered around the hotel swimming pool. Not one sign of the anacondas, jaguars, or monkeys that he'd hoped to find showing off for him from the tops of knotty branches.

Nor was the vegetation how he'd imagined it; by no means did the picture correspond to his idea of the jungle. There were no trees blocking the light of the sun, no vines, no orchids flowering from the crevices in the tree trunks. Instead, what he found was a thick, unvarying mass of vegetation covered in dust from the highway traffic and no more than fifteen or twenty feet in height—a tangle of stunted trees and creepers that looked more like overgrown weeds than tropical jungle.

He was driving south on the highway that stretches along the eastern coast of Yucatán and connects the towns along the Riviera Maya. With the window rolled down and his elbow resting on top of it, he divided his attention between the road and the sky. He studied the bank of clouds over to the east above the island of Cozumel, looking for any change in them, clouds identical to those he'd seen over the last few days—greenish at the bottom, innocuous-looking, and in no way suggestive of an advancing hurricane.

Two hours earlier, his father-in-law had pounded on the door to the room where Joanes, his wife, and his daughter were packing their suitcases.

"Let's grab a sauna," he said when Joanes opened the door. "We'll loosen up a bit and forget all about this damn hurricane."

It was more an order than an invitation. This was how his father-in-law asked for things.

"Do we have time?"

On the edge of the conversation, Joanes's wife went on folding and putting away their clothes, and his father-in-law directed his comments exclusively to Joanes. He knew he was trapped.

"Sure we do!" his father-in-law burst out. His rotund figure, six feet in height and weighing two hundred and sixty pounds, filled the doorframe. "Let's take a sauna. Then we'll file onto those damn busses and get out of here."

The busses were going to transfer the hotel guests to new lodgings in Valladolid, further inland on the peninsula, where they'd stay until the hurricane had passed.

"I still have to get my things together," said Joanes.

But his father-in-law wasn't going to let him get away. He answered as if he hadn't heard him.

"Move your ass! I already greased the sauna guy's palm. He's scramming, too, and I had a hard time convincing him to heat up the sauna so late."

The sauna was, in fact, a typical Mexican *temazcal* sweat lodge. Right next to the pool, there was a small, dome-shaped adobe construction that looked like an igloo or a bread oven. You entered by a door so tiny you had to crawl in on all fours, so tiny the father-in-law's great carcass almost got stuck in it. From outside, Joanes spent a moment staring at that fat, tanned, waxed ass, only partially covered by its yellow Speedo, fighting its way through the door, then he averted his gaze. With considerable effort, huffing and puffing, pleas for help, and reproaches directed at the *temazcalero* who was inside preparing the fire, his father-in-law finally squeezed through the door.

Inside, the roof was little more than three feet high. Joanes and his father-in-law settled themselves as best they could on the bench skirting the circular wall. On the ground, the *temazcalero* stoked the wood fire before placing a few porous stones over the burning logs. Once they were well and truly piping, he poured an infusion of aromatic herbs over them, releasing an eruption of steam.

"You done?" asked Joanes's father-in-law.

"Yes, sir."

"Then leave us to it."

"I'm supposed to control the steam, sir."

"Forget about it. Leave us in private."

"But it's part of the custom," insisted the *temazcalero*.

"So I have to pay you to take a hike, too, do I? Get out of here. I'll tell you when we're done."

The *temazcalero* balked and then slipped out through the tiny door. Once they were alone, Joanes's father-in-law smiled and placed a moist hand on his son-in-law's shoulder.

"How's all that going?"

Joanes, sweating and with his head bent and his elbows resting on his knees, looked up.

"How's what going?"

13

"Your thing. The deal you've got going on."

Joanes looked at him through the cloud of steam. He had absolutely no desire to answer.

"My daughter told me everything," his father-in-law explained.

Joanes could guess what had happened. His father-in-law would have employed his usual interrogation strategy—a well-shaken cocktail of paternal concern, inquisitorial interest, petulance, and overbearingness. And she'd have been left no option but to sling the beast a hunk of meat to appease him. What with her father having supported them financially over the past several years, she had no choice. And what's more, he had covered the cost of this trip, a trip that neither Joanes, his wife, nor their daughter had wanted to take.

Joanes's father-in-law was a painter. His work was sufficiently well recognized that two of his paintings formed part of the Saatchi collection. Oil paintings in earthen tones were his forte; he plastered the canvas with ochre hues, reds and browns, uniformly colored areas, then played with the texture by mixing gravel and bits of bark and small twigs in with the paint. On top of all of this, he would fix a few small, felt squares and rectangles of black, gray, or white. The result, when you looked at it from far enough away, evoked aerial photographs of devastated or deserted landscapes where the rectangles looked like the outlines of edifices lost in the earthy immensity. The color of the felt cuttings, the number of them, and the way in which they were distributed on the canvas defined the different phases of his work.

Six months earlier, the celebrated painter and widower of ten years had surprised the family with the announcement of his sudden engagement to be married.

He'd met a girl in the tanning salon where he went twice a week. She worked there. At the end of each session, she would go into the individual rooms with disinfectant spray and a roll of paper towels and clean the sun bed for the next customer. She was twenty years his junior, didn't have a clue about painting, had a subscription to a personalized online horoscope site, and held a lifelong dream of getting married in Cancún with the turquoise blue of the Caribbean as a backdrop.

"What can you do," his father-in-law had said, shrugging his shoulders. "The girl has a whim."

A few days later, he'd called to let them know that they'd chosen a date for the wedding and that he'd reserved flights and hotel rooms for everyone. It was going to be an intimate affair. Immediate family only. He'd pay for everything. The wedding was set for the end of August, when it would be summer vacation for both his granddaughter and his daughter, who taught philosophy of science at a university. Last but not least, he took it as a given that his son-in-law could put any obligations to his floundering air conditioning business on hold for a few days.

The ceremony and subsequent reception had been a succession of kitsch scenes all teeth-grindingly tasteless for anyone with the slightest aesthetic sensibility. The pièce de résistance had been the arrival of the cake, which came down from the ceiling on a platform, accompanied by a carefully choreographed laser show.

The hurricane alert came that very night. The newlyweds had arranged for themselves and their guests to stay on in Cancún for a few days, but under the new circumstances had decided to change that plan. They hadn't, however, counted on the crush of tourists, all of them desperate to fly out, sending the airport into a total meltdown. There'd been no way to move up their return flight.

Joanes wiped the sweat from his brow, putting off answering. His father-in-law seemed to have expanded in the heat, his butt cheeks spilling over the brick bench.

"We still haven't signed the contract," he said.

His father-in-law said nothing and waited for details.

"There are still a few points to clear up."

"My daughter says that everything that needed to be cleared up already has been."

"Not exactly."

"What's the problem?"

Joanes held in a sigh.

"It's a complicated deal."

"Lucrative, too, according to my daughter."

Joanes nodded. A brief, understated gesture, barely visible in the pungent steam.

"I'd like you to be a little more specific," his father-in-law asked.

"I'd prefer not to talk about it for now."

"You think I don't know that? But I'm concerned about the well-being of my daughter and granddaughter, so tell me something I want to hear."

"You don't need to be concerned about your daughter or granddaughter."

"Don't tell me what should or should not concern me, sonny."

"So let it concern you all you want, just let me take care of them."

The father-in-law leaned in toward him.

"Sonny, *you* can't afford for *me* to not take care of them. When are you going to sign the contract?"

"It's in their hands."

"Soon?"

"Soon."

"That's more like it. Now, clarify 'soon.'"

"Weeks. Or days. It might have already been wrapped up if I hadn't had to come to your wedding."

The father-in-law took this blow without so much as batting an eyelid.

"Weeks or days," he said, chewing over the words. "Do you need me to throw you a bone till then? I can whip you up a couple of paintings. It won't take me long. At this stage in the game, I can do them with my eyes closed."

That was how his father-in-law helped them—with paintings that they then sold. He would show up at their house unannounced, rest the canvas ceremoniously against the back of the sofa, and wait for the family's response, in particular that of his son-in-law. Expressing an opinion on modern art was, for Joanes, like having to speak in some unknown foreign language. His incomprehension couldn't be blamed solely on his limited artistic knowledge, rather it was rooted in the very depths of his being. It didn't help that all his father-in-law's works looked the same to him, nor did his incredulity and irritation at the price fetched for a few depressing, monotonous paintings that crumbled away like the façade of an old building and left his sofa covered in gravel and spongy, paint-soaked wood chips. Under the delighted gaze of his father-in-law, Joanes did his best to say something that wouldn't come across as altogether dumb and could also pass for a thank you.

"No problem," his father-in-law would respond, patting him on the back. Then he would kiss his daughter and granddaughter and leave again, triumphant.

A few days later he would call to find out how much they'd sold the painting for, and without fail, no matter what the amount, he would find it insultingly low. Then he'd rant and rave, insisting he didn't know why he bothered trying to help when they were determined to undersell his work, whose value they either failed to acknowledge or were incapable of appreciating. Finally, he would vow never to give them another painting.

Until a few months later, when he'd turn up at their house, a new canvas in hand.

"Thanks," said Joanes, "but there's no need."

"You sure?"

Joanes nodded and looked away from his father-in-law, who now had torrents of sweat pouring from his shoulders and belly.

The sound of hurried steps and voices could be heard on the other side of the adobe wall. The hotel staff and guests were making their final preparations for the evacuation. The hurricane, named Gerald by the Miami Meteorology Service, was approaching Mexico, picking up energy from the mild Caribbean waters. If their predictions were right, the hurricane would hit the Yucatán peninsula near the island of Cozumel. By this point it would be a Category 2 on the Saffir-Simpson scale. It was expected that after hitting land, it would then shift northeast, sweeping the coastline before heading off into the Golf of Mexico. The Civil Guard declared an orange alert; the hurricane would reach land within the next 24 hours, by tomorrow afternoon.

"How are your girls?" his father-in-law asked. "Nervous?"

"More like mad because they can't go home. And your wife?"

"She's spent the afternoon glued to her computer, chatting with her astrologer. She thinks the hurricane is a bad omen for our marriage."

Joanes refrained from commenting.

"I've spoken to the receptionist," said the father-in-law. From what it looks like, this hotel they're sending us to doesn't exactly have rooms to spare. We're going to have to share."

"Who?"

"The five of us. Two double beds and a cot for the girl," he added.

Joanes wiped more sweat from his face.

"It'll only be for a few days," he said, speaking more to himself than to his father-in-law, who guffawed then cleared his throat and spat on the stones that were topping the fire. His spittle evaporated into steam.

"I doubt it very much, sonny. The receptionist told me that the hotels along the coast are basically uninhabitable after a hurricane. And the last two times, the Cancún airport was out of service for quite a while. A whole bunch of tourists were trapped in the evacuation hotels for weeks. And they were the lucky guys. Others were forced to stay in schools, garages, warehouses . . ."

Joanes couldn't listen to any more. He crawled outside without so much as a goodbye. His father-in-law asked him where in the hell he thought he was going and demanded he come back inside, but Joanes didn't pay him any attention.

He stood leaning against the adobe dome. After the steam bath, even the suffocating air outside seemed cool. Inside the oven, his father-in-law, who couldn't get through the tiny door by himself, shouted for help. Two maintenance men looked at Joanes. One of them asked if everything was all right, and he nodded. They were working next to the pool. The water had been drained to a third of its usual depth and sun loungers and other waterproof furniture had been tossed into it. It would all be better protected from the wind and the rain there than in any other place.

His wife and daughter were quarrelling and didn't even notice when he entered the room. His wife was waving a piece of paper in front of the girl's face. It was a document from the hotel outlining the safety measures they were supposed to take.

"It says here that in the event of a hurricane, you have to dress in white."

"Mom, I refuse to wear anything white. It's a matter of principles. You know this," said the girl unequivocally. "I don't even own anything white. Not even panties."

"I can lend you something of mine."

The girl's bangs fell over her eyes. She flicked them aside in a theatrical gesture of boredom. Her hair was black and shone like a beetle's armor. She was wearing a T-shirt (also black), denim cut-offs (her only concession to the tropical climate), and some fuchsia Converse sneakers decorated with hand-drawn, black flies. She closed her eyes and slowly shook her head. The request was completely non-negotiable.

Realizing this, her mother huffed and turned, and that's when she noticed her husband.

"Back already? Did the sauna help you unwind a little?"

"Not exactly."

"Dad, you're soaked," said the girl, with a look of repulsion. "Don't you wanna, like, take a shower or something?"

"Sure do," he said, and went into the bathroom. He emerged a few minutes later, patting himself dry with a towel he then flung into a corner. He put on the first polo shirt he came across in his heap of clothes and grabbed his wallet, his satellite cell phone, and the car keys.

"Where are you going?" asked his wife. "The busses are coming to pick us up in a couple of hours."

"I need to get some air. Throw the rest of my things together, will you please?"

And before leaving, he added, "I'll be back in time."

A minute later, he was on the road.

He was driving along a monotonous, straight stretch of road when his phone rang. Before answering he made a mental calculation of the time in Spain. Just after eleven at night.

"We have to talk," said a deep, male voice.

It was the same voice that, over the last several months, had become as familiar to him as his wife and daughter's. The voice seemed astonishingly close. He noted the graveness in it, which unnerved him. This wasn't the time for graveness. Each and every point in the agreement had been clearly laid out, had been revised, reconsidered, re-written, and revised again.

He felt his back tense up. He drove with one hand on the wheel and his eyes fixed on the horizon where all the highway lanes converged in a single vanishing point.

"All right, let's talk. Is there a problem?"

The second the question slipped out, he regretted it, as if the mere mention of a problem were enough to invoke one.

"There is, in fact," said the voice. "Something's come up."

"I thought everything had been agreed on."

"I mean *someone* has come up."

A long pause.

"His price and conditions are pretty interesting. I've just received an offer."

Another pause.

"You see, kid, I like your numbers, but I'd be lying if I said that these guys haven't impressed me."

"Who's the offer from?"

"You know it would be wrong to tell you."

"And you know that I can find out without your help."

"So find out."

Another pause. Joanes took a deep breath.

"What are they offering?" he asked.

"I can't tell you that, either."

"Oh, come on . . ."

"More or less the same as you, but for a better price."

Joanes swore under his breath. He didn't have any margin left for further discounts. If he lowered the price, he'd lose money.

"Well then?" he said, gathering all the strength he could. "What happens now?"

"You seem trustworthy, kid, you really do," came the voice at the other end of the line, "but we're going to have to review your offer."

"What do you want to review? There's nothing to review. And anyhow, I'm in Mexico. They're evacuating us because of the hurricane. You must have heard about it on the news."

The voice spoke again, and this time the graveness had an added dose of testiness to it—the last thing the man wanted to hear about were other people's problems; he had more than enough of his own.

"Listen up, our decision is now between your offer and the one I've just received. And, to be honest, the balance is tipping toward the latter. We want to settle the matter as soon as possible. We're meeting tomorrow to make a decision."

"Who are you meeting with? I thought it was up to you."

"It's never up to one person alone. Less still when there's so much money in the mix."

"Well that's the impression you've always given me."

"Wait for our call tomorrow," said the voice, now curt. "We'll let you know what we decide."

"Call me before the meeting," Joanes said. "I'll review my offer tonight. Improve it."

"In all honesty, I don't think it'll make any difference."

"You owe it to me."

"I don't owe you a thing. Don't be under any false illusions."

"You'll call?"

"I'm not promising."

"So then I'll call you. I'll find a way to drop the price."

"No. I'll call you," said the voice before hanging up.

He switched on his emergency blinkers and pulled over to the shoulder, a ramshackle strip of road full of rubble and trash and barely a foot and a half wide, which was all the distance that existed between the road and the nearby undergrowth. He closed his eyes and leaned back against the headrest. He thought about what would happen if his offer was rejected. It wasn't just months of negotiations at stake but the entire future of his company.

He stayed there for a long time, not caring that his family was waiting for him to go to the shelter. Double-trailer trucks and pickups filled with laborers drove past, just inches from the car. Not even their honking made him open his eyes.

"Don't panic," he said out loud. "You're going to work it out. Go back to the hotel."

And he repeated, "Don't panic."

And again, "Don't panic."

He checked to make sure there weren't any vehicles approaching and made a U-turn, driving right over the median, when a figure appeared from the undergrowth and hurled itself onto the highway in front of the car. For a second he thought it was a kid, a black kid. It appeared at the edge his field of vision then stumbled onto the highway, walking strangely, swaying with its arms up in the air, as if trying to catch someone's attention to get them to stop. But Joanes was too close, and the car was going too fast. The bumper hit the figure hard, slamming it forward and sending it rolling several yards over the asphalt.

Joanes slammed on the brakes and looked in shock at the sorry figure. The fact that it was covered in hair did little to calm him down. It wasn't a kid but a monkey.

He got out of the car and walked toward it cautiously. It was a chimpanzee. He asked himself what in God's name a chimpanzee was doing there. He thought they only existed in equatorial Africa. It began to sidle off, and Joanes stopped in his tracks.

The monkey got to its feet slowly, threw a pained look at Joanes, and hobbled off the highway. It disappeared back into the thicket from which it had emerged.

He had no idea what to do. A few vehicles drove by, but they didn't pay him any attention. Nobody had witnessed the accident.

He decided to go after the chimpanzee.

He imagined it would leave some sort of trail—footprints, a path crushed through the vegetation or something—but as soon as he entered the undergrowth, it was impossible to make out anything. He went on anyhow, battling his way through the low branches and vines, changing tack every now and then and retracing his steps various times. He shooed away some iguanas resting among the roots of the trees; they moved off, making a crunching sound in the leaves. He only found the monkey because it hadn't had the strength to get far. Joanes pushed aside a curtain of hanging vines and was suddenly face to face with it.

It was sitting on the ground, leaning against a tree and cradling the arm the car had hit. It was a female, and she was wearing a collar with a metal jump ring hanging off it. When she saw Joanes, she held out her other hand to him pitifully, opening and closing her fingers, entreating him to come closer. Her chest rose and fell in a painful motion. Joanes hesitated. He knew chimpanzees to be capable of a degree of ferocity totally at odds with their cuddly image. But this one didn't seem to be in a state to hurt anyone, and the collar suggested that she was used to human company.

Joanes knelt down and took her hand. With her eyes half closed, the chimpanzee looked at him and moved her lips as if she wanted to say something or give him a kiss. She seemed well advanced in age. Her forehead was bald, and the hair on her shoulders and back was gray, as were the hairs on her chin and the ends of her fingers. More than pain, her eyes—deep-set and wrinkly—revealed immense exhaustion.

The chimpanzee held Joanes's hand to her chest, as if she wanted to feel him closer, and he didn't resist. The animal held on to his hand as her breathing slowed. Not long after, she closed her eyes, and her head fell to one side.

Even so, Joanes didn't let go of her. He remained still for a moment until he, too, closed his eyes and bowed his head. Holding on to the body of the chimpanzee, surrounded by that thickset jungle where nobody could see or hear him, he broke down in tears. He let the tears flood out, until his throat hurt from so much crying. In between sobs, he coughed, spluttered, and spat out curses and insults, many of them directed at himself.

Afterward, he slowly freed his hand from the chimp's. He inspected the collar, hoping to find some sort of identification. There wasn't any. The monkey had a bracelet on her right wrist, a little trinket made of pink and blue plastic beads. The kind of charm a little girl might wear.

He was wiping away his tears when the phone rang. He cleared his throat and took a deep breath before answering.

"Where are you?" asked his wife, clearly anxious. "The busses are here."

"I've had a little accident."

"Are you OK?"

"Yes."

"Are you sure?"

"Yes, it's no big deal."

"What happened?"

"I'll tell you later."

"But you're OK."

"Absolutely."

"And what about the evacuation?"

"You two go on ahead with your dad and the others."

"And you?"

"I'm staying."

There was a pause, then she said she didn't understand.

"I'm staying," he repeated. "I'll catch up later. On my own. I'll see you in Valladolid."

"Today? You'll come today?"

27

He told her no, that he'd spend the night in the hotel and leave the following morning, once he'd gotten some rest. Before his wife had a chance to object, he added that the wind wasn't going to hit until the afternoon. If he set off at sunrise, he'd have more than enough time to get there.

"You should really think about this."

"I told you, I'm staying."

There was another pause, and then she said, "Fine. Just be careful."

In the background, Joanes could hear his father-in-law grumbling away.

"What's your dad's problem now?"

"He wants to know what time you're going to arrive."

"Gee, it's nice to hear he's concerned about me for once."

"Yes, well. I'll call you tonight, from Valladolid."

"Did you turn in my computer for the hotel staff to keep safe?"

"I was going to do it now."

"Leave it in the room. Since I'm staying, I'll use it to go over some things."

"Is there some kind of problem?" she asked.

And lowering her voice, she added, "Is it work?"

"No. I just want to go over a couple of things, for my own peace of mind."

"Are you sure you're OK?"

"Of course! We'll talk later, when things are calmer."

He went back to the car to look for something he could dig a grave with. On opening the trunk, he realized why his father-in-law had been so concerned. His golf clubs were inside. Clearly, he'd wanted to put them in a safe place before leaving for the evacuation hotel, where, in order to speed up the relocation process, nobody was allowed to take any large pieces of luggage.

He picked the club used for getting out of sand bunkers. It had a smooth, iron head fashioned at a sharp angle, about forty degrees, to the shaft. He returned to the chimpanzee. In that same spot, he began to dig the grave, using the exorbitant golf club alternately as a shovel and a pick. The earth was spongy, damp, and perfumed, and bright black like caviar. But it was also intertwined with roots he had to work around or, if they were small, break up with his hands or by hitting them with the club. He spent hours digging a grave big and deep enough.

He carefully laid the body down, in a posture he deemed somewhat dignified. He used his hands to push the dirt back on top of it. He would have liked to cover the tomb with stones, so that no vermin could pull the body out. But there were no stones around other than bits of highway rubble, which were too small and, in some inexplicable way, didn't seem appropriate. And so he called it a day.

Dragging the club along behind him, Joanes returned to the car. He was soaked in sweat and caked in dirt from head to toe, and his hands were covered in cuts and scrapes. He wanted to scream away his frustration and rage. He felt like pounding the car with the club, the car rented with his father-in-law's money, the car with which he'd hit that poor animal. He wanted to dent the hood. To smash the windshield to smithereens.

Instead, he simply stood contemplating the club with contempt and let it slide through his fingers. It landed in among the plastic bottles, cigarette butts, and sun-bleached bits of paper that littered the shoulder of the highway.

The icy wind made their eyes water, and they had to hold on to their helmets to prevent them from flying off. They weaved in and out of the workers that were swarming all over the place on that floor, and Joanes and his host approached the security rail. Their position, pretty high up, and the air, clear now because of the wind, meant they could see far into the distance. The blue sea turned a tone darker beyond the line that skirted the coast, where the sea floor plummeted to far greater depths.

"What do you make of that?" asked his host, his voice deep and serene.

"Spectacular."

"I happen to think so. Right there," he said, pointing to the bare, concrete floor, "is where we're putting one of the suites, and here," he added, pointing to the empty space in front of them, "a floor-to-ceiling window. This view deserves nothing less."

He emphasized his words with an imaginary stroke of the blue horizon.

"Those are going to be the apartment blocks."

He was referring to three skeleton structures that had been built just a little farther up the coast, next to the site on which they were currently standing.

Joanes admired the panorama in silence. His tie flapped in the wind. Above him there was nothing but cyanotic blue sky.

He hadn't felt this good in ages. If everything went according to plan, he would also be handling the apartment blocks. But he stopped himself from thinking that far ahead. He needed to focus on the task at hand, an upcoming hotel with one hundred and fifteen rooms for which he'd be providing the air conditioning— one individual unit in each room, wiring, boilers, air conditioners, air quality control systems . . .

"Do you think you can take care of it?" asked his host and potential client.

"Absolutely."

"Pleased to hear it, because I can assure you that all this is just the tip of the iceberg."

PART II

Hotel

By the time he got back to the hotel, the buses had already been gone for hours. He entered the lobby carrying the golf clubs. The manager stopped him, clearly alarmed by his appearance and late arrival. Joanes calmed him down, assuring him that he was fine and promising he wouldn't be staying to see the hurricane. Even so, he had to sign a disclaimer to the effect that he had declined to leave the hotel with his fellow guests.

His wife had gotten everything in order. The family's luggage had been wrapped in the plastic bags provided by the hotel and placed on the highest shelves in the closet. She'd left his clothes for the following day on the bed. Despite his exhaustion, Joanes couldn't help smiling at the little row of things neatly laid out—a change of underwear, a rain jacket, his passport, a road map, a small first-aid kit, a note giving the address and telephone number of the evacuation hotel, and a backpack to keep it all in.

He dropped the golf clubs in a corner of the room and took a long shower. Afterward, he took one of the suitcases from the closet, removed the sticky tape on its bag, and pulled out some clean clothes.

He ate dinner in the hotel restaurant. A sour-faced waiter in plain clothes served him. Save for Joanes, the place was empty, and with the best part of the furniture stowed away, it was pretty depressing.

He was back in his room, working on his laptop, when the landline rang.

"How are you?" his wife asked.

Joanes threw himself onto the bed to talk. The TV was muted and tuned to a news channel.

"I'm fine. What about you guys?"

"Fine," she answered wearily.

"Sure?"

"I'm fine now that I've finally gotten a moment to myself. The others are eating downstairs. They've given us a spot on the fourth canteen shift."

"You're not eating?"

"I'd rather talk to you. Tell me what happened."

He told her about hitting the chimpanzee.

"What was a chimpanzee doing on the highway?"

"I don't know."

He told her how he'd looked for the dying animal in the undergrowth, and how he's stayed with it until it died, and how afterward he'd felt the need to bury it. He didn't tell her he'd cried.

"That's why you didn't get back in time?"

"That's why, yeah."

"Nothing else has happened?"

"No, nothing."

He didn't see the point, for now, in telling her about the problems with the contract.

She sighed.

"You think I was wrong."

"What?"

35

"Spending all that time burying it. Burying her, I should say. She was a female."

"I don't know. I suppose it was the right thing to do. But I hope you'll come soon."

"Of course I will. You guys are OK, right? You're with your dad."

"Yes. And my stepmom. I'm going to share a room with my stepmom. You've got to see the nightie she's brought. I've seen windows less transparent."

Joanes laughed.

"The later it gets, the more I want to get there."

After a pause she said, "All of this is so weird. The hurricane, the monkey on the highway . . ."

He agreed with her.

"What's the place like?"

She gave a snort. Both the evacuation hotel and the town itself were in absolute chaos. More and more relocated tourists kept showing up, and Mexican people, too. There wasn't a single bed left in all of Valladolid. In complete contrast to what they'd seen in Cancún, the hotels hadn't prepared at all for the hurricane. They all trusted that where they were, it wouldn't do any more harm than a regular storm. The hoteliers were making the most of the situation. Those without a reservation were willing to pay any amount for a room; the hoteliers pocketed the money and put them in the spaces reserved for evacuees. As a result, the tourists coming from the coast wound up sleeping on mats in the common areas.

Joanes heard his wife yawn.

"You should go and eat something and rest. I'll see you in the morning."

"In the morning," she repeated. "Please be careful."

"Don't worry."

"I love you."

"Me too."

"Sure?"

"Of course I'm sure."

The silence in the room was unbearable after they hung up. Joanes looked for the remote control and turned up the volume on the TV.

A minute later he muted it again.

He went on working for a few hours. Afterward, he jotted down the changes he'd have to make to his offer in a little notebook. Before going to bed, he put the notebook in the backpack he'd take with him the following day.

He was up and about before sunrise. He put the suitcase he'd opened back up in the closet and sealed the doors with tape. He made sure he had everything his wife had left out for him, as well as water and food for the journey.

The moment he stepped out of the room, a maid and two maintenance men hurtled in. It seemed as if they'd spent the night in the hallway, waiting for him to open the door. They began stripping the bed, removing electrical appliances, and transferring as much furniture as they could from the bedroom to the bathroom.

"Wait a minute, sir."

The maid had come after him, carrying the golf clubs.

"What about these?"

Joanes shrugged.

"Do whatever you want with them."

The hotel seemed totally different. Everything had been organized for the hurricane's arrival. The furniture, lamps, and decorative pieces from the hallways and common areas had been removed. The insides of the windows and glass doors were taped from corner to corner with big crosses. In the courtyard, the trees had had their coconuts cut off and their branches strapped down with metal bands so that the wind wouldn't rip them off.

Joanes handed in his laptop at reception and took a receipt in exchange.

"Good luck," said the receptionist, by way of goodbye.

There wasn't a cloud in the sky. Nothing in the air suggested that the day would be any less sunny and calm than the previous ones. And yet that impression stood in stark relief to the Cancún hotel strip, which looked like a ghost town. Most of the hotels had already relocated their guests.

After merging onto the highway for Valladolid, he realized that the local population had also prepared for the hurricane. The repair shops, car dealers, and spare part depots that flanked the highway outside of Cancún for several miles had their doors and windows boarded up and their signs taken down.

He soon found himself in an increasingly dense flow of vehicles, which, like him, were heading further into the peninsular for shelter. His car joined a motley caravan of passenger cars, buses, motorcycles, and construction and farming vehicles. He spotted pickups carrying various generations of the same family, most of whom were crammed into the back, shielded by awnings made of tube frames covered in plastic sheets or palm leaves. He saw a digger moving along with its bucket raised high and three kids sitting inside it surrounded by backpacks and bundles of clothes. He also saw busses evacuating tourists. He exchanged resigned looks with the passengers inside them.

The traffic slowed to a desperate crawl, not helped by various fender benders or by the two military checkpoints where soldiers with machine guns were halting vehicles and even ordering a few onto the shoulder. Once there, the passengers were forced to get out while a pair of Rottweilers sniffed the vehicle and rummaged around in the mountains of bags and suitcases that made up their luggage.

Try as he might not to, Joanes glanced every few minutes at the clock.

"Are you going to keep us here all day?" he asked aloud to himself after almost an hour spent blocked at the second checkpoint.

The previous afternoon, he'd gone to a store to buy food for the journey. Panic buying had laid the place to waste. In the canned food aisle, he'd found just a few dented cans. He'd grabbed a couple of the most presentable among them and a loaf of sliced bread. The bottles of water were rationed to two per customer.

He started in on his scant provisions out of sheer boredom.

The sky was still clear.

The highway here cut through thicker and taller vegetation than he'd seen on the coast. He found he was able to put his foot down a little along those stretches of road with more lanes, but even so, the average speed along the way was painfully slow.

He was driving along a straight stretch when, in the distance, he spied two people on the shoulder. One of the figures was standing watching the traffic. The other was sitting on something he couldn't make out. It looked like they might be hitchhiking, and yet they weren't making any effort to catch the attention of the passing vehicles; instead, they just stood there, unmoving. When he drove past them, he saw that it was a man and a woman; she was in a wheelchair. Joanes's eyes met the man's for a fraction of a second.

He continued on some twenty or thirty yards before slamming on the brakes. The car behind had no choice but to swerve violently to avoid crashing into him. The driver showed his irritation with a long honk of his horn. Joanes moved to the shoulder, where he sat stock-still, his hands on the wheel, staring into his rearview mirror at the two figures behind him.

The man, in fact an elderly gentleman, was now looking in the direction of the car. The woman, wearing a straw hat, hadn't changed her stance at all, her body was hunched and her head bent.

But all of Joanes's attention was fixed on him. On the elderly gentleman.

He was wearing slacks and a short-sleeved, white, button-down shirt. He'd put on a good number of pounds. What had once been a stout stomach was now a serious belly hanging over his belt. The man's double chin was now a triple. And the large, square-framed, black-rimmed glasses reminiscent of old TV sets had now been replaced by a more modern pair. But his imperious air was the same as ever.

The elderly man moved guardedly toward the car. Joanes got out.

"Hello," he said.

"A compatriot!" responded the man with great satisfaction, holding out his hand.

As he took it, Joanes scrutinized his face, but there was nothing in it to suggest that the other man recognized him.

"Hello, professor."

The old man's smile immediately vanished.

"I don't think you remember me. I was your student. At the School of Engineering.

He added his name and the year it had been.

The professor looked at him, creasing his forehead, and shook his head.

"I'm sorry," he said. "I don't remember you. But in any case, I'm incredibly pleased to see you."

"What's happened?"

The professor pursed his lips.

"We've been the victims of a mutiny," he said, containing his rage. "We were on the bus, on our way to one of those shelters, when the other passengers ganged up against me and my wife, forcing us to get off. They threw us out. Kicked us to the curb and then just went on their way. We should be thankful they didn't hurt us."

Joanes shook his head, confused.

"But, why?"

"Intolerance, my friend. Because they gave in to the irritation produced by a minor inconvenience and let their nerves get the better of them. Because of her condition, my wife requires a little more space than other people. A hard, narrow, straight-backed seat is terribly tiring for her. This fact, in a bus with more passengers than seats and a faulty air-conditioning system, was enough to incite the uprising."

"And there was no one to defend you? A hotel rep, the driver . . . ?"

The professor gave an emphatic shake of the head.

"Only the driver, but the last thing he wanted was to get involved. He obeyed those savages without so much as a word when they ordered him to stop. Just imagine the scene. They lifted my wife up in midair and set her on the curb! As if she were a piece of luggage!"

"Is that your wife over there?" Joanes asked, pointing to the woman in the wheelchair.

"Forgive me. I should have introduced you. My manners are melting in this heat."

Joanes followed him to where his wife was sitting.

"Darling, you won't believe the stroke of luck we've had!"

When her husband introduced her to Joanes, she simply looked at him meekly. She barely shifted the pained look on her face, as if smiling took an unbearable effort. Her eyebrows were plucked bald, and her dress—white, no belt or frills—looked like a hospital gown. When the professor added that Joanes had been a student of his, her response was, "In that case, I'm not sure we are so lucky."

A trailer whizzed past, and she shut her eyes tight to protect them from the dust.

"Where was the bus supposed to be taking you?" asked Joanes.

"I don't know," answered the professor. "I heard someone say the name of the city, but . . ."

"I'm going to Valladolid."

"That could be the place. I think it might have been, yes."

"Would you like me to take you?"

The professor replied with an enormous smile and shook his hand again, now more firmly than before.

"You can't imagine how grateful we'd be if you would. I didn't dare ask you myself."

"It's not a problem. But we ought to get going. It's already a little late."

Joanes watched as the professor threw his travel bag over his shoulder and pushed his wife toward the car. The chair was motorized, but she needed help there along the rubbly shoulder.

The whole story about the mutiny on the bus seemed strange to Joanes. He found it hard to believe that the other passengers would have thrown them off the bus simply because of a space issue. Something else had gone on, surely. The professor must have provoked the others somehow, which, knowing him, wasn't hard to imagine.

They settled the woman into the back seat and put the wheelchair in the trunk.

Joanes sat down at the wheel but didn't turn on the engine right away. He wanted to fix that place firmly in his memory—that nasty stretch of Mexican highway, the roadside hawk perched and watching them from a signpost . . .

He had imagined this moment countless times since leaving college. In his fantasies, the professor always appeared in some desperate situation where he had no choice but to ask Joanes for help, recognizing, implicitly, that he'd made a terrible mistake in underestimating him as he had. And Joanes always helped him out, making a point of being sober and efficient. He'd make it clear that things were going great, that he ran a prosperous business, that he had an enviable family, and, ultimately, that the professor's harmful influence hadn't had the least effect on him.

"Is something wrong?" asked the professor.

"No, nothing," answered Joanes, starting up the engine. "Everything's in order."

The professor belonged to a family of dentists. His grandfather, father, and two of his uncles had all practiced dentistry. Out of all of them all, the professor's father had enjoyed the most prolific career, having made a small fortune from the patents of various professional instruments—two endodontic clamps, a drill burr, a barbed broach, and, most significantly, a dental milling cutter universally praised by his colleagues in the field.

The professor's students liked to point out the appropriateness of him being part of a family who'd made their money inflicting pain on others, and they considered the professor's move from dentistry to teaching math as a sign of his loyalty to the family tradition, and his personal refinement of it.

He specialized in algorithm theory and recursive mathematical functions and was not exactly up there among the most popular professors in the School of Engineering. He owed his less than favorable reputation to the excessive demands he placed on his students, along with his penchant for upsetting and intimidating them, inciting such levels of insecurity that, for a few, the problem became congenital.

In one of the first of the professor's classes Joanes attended, the former took the whole lecture hall by surprise with an inflammatory speech defending the duodecimal system. According to him, various strong cases could be made for replacing the modern decimal system with a duodecimal one. Calculations would become far easier, he assured them. Multiplication and division would be far more practicable, owing to the duodecimal system having four factors—two, three, four, and six—while the decimal system, to its detriment, only had two—two and five. Another of the arguments he put forward was the widespread acceptance—both historical and geographical—of a base 12 numeral system, as demonstrated by the existence of the twelve signs of the zodiac, the division of the year into twelve months, and of the foot into twelve inches. He concluded by pointing out—in case more or clearer explications were necessary—that human anatomy lends itself to counting in divisions of twelve—four of their fingers have three phalanges, and four times three is twelve. The thumb serves as a pointer when counting the phalanges on the other fingers.

"Think about it," he told them.

A few days later, the professor asked them if they'd thought about what he'd said. The first voices in favor piped up timidly. But many others soon jumped on the bandwagon, expressing their approval for the duodecimal system and chipping in with new reasons to support it. The professor listened with a satisfied smirk on his face. After a while, the room fell silent. All eyes were on him as the students waited to hear what he would say about the lively response his speech had inspired. But rather than adding anything, he burst out laughing, and his laugh reverberated through the room like the sound of stone scratching stone.

"You are bunch of idiots," he told the students. "How could you possibly think that I consider the signs of the zodiac or the twelve moons of the year to be just reasons for changing our elegant numeral system?"

And he repeated.

"Idiots."

Then he added, "And ignoramuses."

By that point, he'd stopped laughing, and his face was puce.

"I fed you that load of nonsense merely to test your critical faculties. And I regret to confirm that you do not possess any such faculties. From this moment on," he cautioned, pointing at them with a threatening finger, "it is your duty to question everything I say from this podium or write on this blackboard. Absolutely everything."

Joanes didn't miss a single day of the professor's Numerical Analysis course. When he was with his friends, he joined in their harsh digs of him. But in his case, it was all an act. What he really felt for the professor was admiration.

This feeling was only amplified by the professor's encyclopedic knowledge (encyclopedic from a student's point of view), his assured, precise manner of teaching, his aristocratic indifference toward his students, and the frequent and prolonged silences into which he fell, sometimes mid-sentence, during which he would stare blankly into the distance, as if the students and everything in the room had vanished into thin air. Often, after one of these silences, he would scribble a few lines in the notebook that he kept in his breast pocket. Then he'd continue the class where he'd left off.

Joanes's admiration of the professor was also fueled by the fame and recognition the man enjoyed in his field, and the impressive row of dog-eared books with his name on the spine that sat in the college library.

On numerous occasions, Joanes tried to get close to the professor, to gain his confidence, but the man's distant character and the school's educational model, which did not allow for contact between faculty and students, rendered any efforts useless. He took out a few of his books from the library and flicked through them fervently, but their contents were too advanced for him. He had to resign himself to simply admiring the beautiful, castle-like configurations of his equations.

All this changed when, in the middle of the course, the professor published a biography of the English mathematician Alan Turing. Turing had been one of the pioneers of computing and was greatly admired by the professor, who often cited him in class. His previous articles had been published in renowned journals in the field. However, his book about Turing, whose title was a pun—*Turing: Pragmatic Mathematics*—was published by a little-known house specialized in texts on chess.

During the professor's routine digressions on Alan Turing, Joanes sensed a level of admiration similar to that which he felt for his don, and on this basis, he thought that the book might hold clues to certain facets of the professor's personality that he kept hidden from his students, information on his tastes and interests. The moment that *Turing: Pragmatic Mathematics* was published, he rushed straight out to buy it.

The book included absolutely no mention of Turing's private life, focusing solely on his professional career. He ran through the most celebrated episodes of that career: the publication of his famous article, "On Computable Numbers," in which Turing postulated the existence of a hypothetical machine—the "a-machine"—which, by applying a finite series of steps, would be capable of determining the veracity or falseness of any affirmation; the mathematician's crucial role in World War II, helping to decipher the Germans' cryptographic codes using the Enigma machine; and his subsequent, failed attempts to bring the a-machine to life.

The last part of *Turing: Pragmatic Mathematics* was somewhat nebulous. Regarding Turing's death, at the tender age of forty-one, the professor made only a fleeting reference to the "lamentable circumstances" in which it had transpired. There then followed a series of reflections—more philosophical than mathematical—on Turing's lasting influence on mathematics and computer science.

Joanes's efforts to get to the bottom of the professor's character had been mostly in vain. The professor clearly admired Turing, but everybody knew that. His enthusiasm was clear from the book's rambling writing style, light years away from the strict precision of the language he used in class and demanded of his students. Joanes wasn't the least surprised that the hagiography that was *Turing: Pragmatic Mathematics* had been published by a minor press. He saw it as a personal whim, a way for the professor to let his hair down, almost like when scientists publish science fiction under pseudonyms.

Given how few conclusions about the professor he'd been able to arrive at by reading what *was* written in *Turing: Pragmatic Mathematics*, Joanes decided to look for some in the things he *hadn't* written. In order to do so, he got ahold of another Turing biography, one that was more comprehensive and not so blatantly partial. He discovered that Turing was an eccentric, known for holding up his pants with a rope instead of a belt and for chaining his teacup to a radiator each night. These behaviors, coupled with his private nature and scant social skills, kept him outside the relevant mathematics circles, where he was looked upon with disdain or, at best, with paternalistic tolerance.

What's more, he was homosexual, and in mid-twentieth-century England, this wasn't to the benefit of anyone's professional career.

In 1952, Turing began a relationship with a young man from Manchester. He was called Arnold Murray, and he was nineteen. Murray's incessant requests for money drove them to a violent argument. A few days later, Murray broke into Turing's house. Turing called the police. The subsequent investigation exposed the kind of relationship the mathematician and the young man shared. In accordance with Section 11 of the Criminal Law Amendment Act of 1885, Turing was accused of gross indecency.

To avoid serving jail time, he agreed to undergo a treatment that would "cure him of his illness." The estrogen injections administered to him as a form of chemical castration had side effects. Turing gained weight and developed breasts.

On the morning of July 8, 1954, Turing's housemaid came across his dead body. He was in bed, and beside him was an apple with several bites taken out of it. A post-mortem examination revealed that the fruit had been laced with cyanide.

From the moment of its first release, Turing had been fascinated by the Disney movie *Snow White and the Seven Dwarves*. One of his little eccentricities was reciting the verse that the evil stepmother spoke as she poisoned the apple she'd later offer to Snow White:

Dip the apple in the brew.
Let the Sleeping Death seep through.

None of this was mentioned in *Turing: Pragmatic Mathematics*. Joanes had previously thought that the professor had simply gotten swept away in the writing of his book, but this new information changed everything. The professor had put himself through a stringent process of self-control in order to divert his focus away from what he considered to be the most reprehensible aspects of Turing's life. Comparing the two texts, Joanes concluded that what most vexed the professor was the weakness of Turing's character, the immature facets of his personality, which had proved so harmful to his work. His immaturity had impeded the pragmatism so admired by the professor, the pragmatism that had first driven Turing to tear through the tough, translucent membrane that separates theory and practice, to abandon the crystal palace of pure mathematics and begin frequenting the workshops where engineers got their hands dirty. And if this so maddened the professor, perhaps it was because he feared that he, too, suffered from the same kind of immaturity, that his private life was an obstacle in the way of his professional life.

And on top of this was the matter of Turing's homosexuality. One might guess that the absolute surgical removal of this topic from *Turing: Pragmatic Mathematics* was owing to the revulsion, or unease, that it awoke in the professor. Joanes fantasized about how perturbed the professor would be by the image of Turing's lifeless corpse—stretched out on the bed with his fingers interlocked atop his stomach, his pajamas stretched across his estrogen-produced breasts, his eyes closed peacefully, as if he were waiting for a prince to come and wake him with a gentle kiss on the lips.

Joanes's readings led him to believe that he knew the professor better than ever, and certainly better than the rest of the students. He saw it as a personal triumph, as if no one else could have read the same books and arrived at similar conclusions. The knowledge that he had insights into what he considered to be the private opinions—and, as such, weak spots—of the professor made Joanes bolder in class. He no longer bowed his head when his eyes met the professor's. He liked to think that the don had noticed what had happened and held him in special regard.

Joanes passed Numerical Analysis with the highest grade in his class. And in his subsequent years at the school, he never lost sight of the professor, regularly crossing paths with him in the School of Engineering. The professor responded to his greetings with dispassionate nods. He didn't seem to remember who Joanes was.

There was only half a bottle of water left, which Joanes offered to the professor's wife. She drank thirstily. Afterward, she dampened a handkerchief and patted her face and neck with it. Her husband then had a drink, after which she hastened to take back the bottle and kept it on her.

The professor asked Joanes what he was doing in Mexico, and Joanes gave him the short version of events.

"So why aren't you with your family?"

Joanes explained that his wife and daughter had gone on ahead and were already in Valladolid. The professor wanted to know the reason why he'd stayed behind, so Joanes explained the episode with the monkey.

"It was wearing a collar. I suppose it must have escaped from somewhere. There are a bunch of theme parks in the area. It's possible at least one of them keeps monkeys. It was wearing a bracelet, too. A cheap little accessory, with blue and pink beads."

"How curious," remarked the professor.

In the rearview mirror, Joanes kept an eye on the woman. Most of the time, she had her eyes closed.

"Are you feeling all right?" he asked her.

She stared at him for a few seconds then said, "Are we very far from the place?"

"I don't know exactly. I don't think so."

She mumbled something unintelligible and closed her eyes again.

The professor looked out at the landscape, an anxious look on his face. Joanes told himself that it would be better to save any questions for later.

The professor had the road map laid out on his lap, and he kept a watchful eye on the road signs. It was past midday when he tutted and drew the map right up to his nose to study it closer.

"Is there a problem?" asked Joanes.

"I've just seen a sign saying how many miles it is to Valladolid."

"And?"

"The number of miles was higher than it said on the last sign."

"Are we lost?" asked the wife.

"No," answered Joanes and the professor in unison.

Though they couldn't be certain. Every crossroad and fork was a chaos of vehicles either joining or exiting the main stream of traffic, to the extent that you couldn't even tell which was the main road. Not long after, they passed a sign that didn't even mention Valladolid. The professor went back to studying the map.

"I think we're somewhere around here," he said, pointing to an area north of the highway that they should have stayed on and which, to all appearances, they'd strayed from without realizing.

"How far from Valladolid?" asked Joanes.

"I don't know. This map covers the whole of Mexico. You should have gotten a detailed one of just the state."

He went back to look at the map again and said that they might be forty miles from Valladolid. Maybe more.

The three of them looked at their watches, then at the sky, which was still clear. Joanes tried to appear calm, although he felt far from it.

He wasn't just worried about how close the hurricane was. He had hoped to have received a call by now from the man who was, up until the day before, an almost sure client. He hadn't told Joanes the exact time the meeting with whoever it was had been scheduled for, but in Spain, seven hours ahead, it was already evening.

He told himself to think positively. Perhaps the meeting had been postponed until the following day. For as long as Joanes had known him, his client had never given him any reason to mistrust him. If he'd said that he'd call, he'd call. Then Joanes would have the chance to explain the markdowns—minimal ones, but markdowns all the same—that he'd applied to his offer.

To top it all off, his phone was nearly out of battery. The night before, busy going over the hotel deal, he'd forgotten to charge it. By the time he realized the next morning, he'd already set off, but he figured that the remaining battery would last him for the rest of the journey. He hadn't counted on the terrible traffic, or on getting lost.

In the run-up to his trip to Mexico, Joanes had rented a satellite telephone. With the hotel contract still in the air, he wanted to be reachable anytime and anyplace. The product description had promised it was designed "for the toughest customer, in the toughest conditions." These words were accompanied by a photo of a soldier in desert gear standing in front of a horizon of sand dunes, talking on the very same phone. But with the battery dead, it wasn't much use to anyone. He regretted now not having asked for the whole accessory pack, which included a spare battery, a charger that connected to the car lighter, and a portable solar panel that would allow the phone to charge without any electricity at all.

"What are we going to do?" asked the professor's wife.

Joanes said that they'd keep going until they came to a sign that would help them get their bearings. But not long after, they found themselves stuck on a stretch of road with a single lane in each direction, both bumper to bumper.

"Now what?" the professor wanted to know.

Joanes looked at his watch again. Then he got out of the car to see how far the backup went on for. A U-turn wasn't possible at the moment, nor was it a particularly appealing option. He made signs to try to catch the attention of the driver in the car that had come to a standstill next to them in the opposite lane. The man was Mexican, and he was eating a slice of pineapple. There was a woman in the passenger seat and four young children in the back. Tied to the car roof was a mattress.

"Which way to Valladolid?"

The Mexican man pulled a puzzled face. He looked ahead of him and then turned back, peering between his children's heads, as if he didn't know where he was, either.

"That way," he said, pointing ahead with his slice of pineapple, in the exact opposite direction from the one Joanes's car was facing.

"Is it far?"

"I don't think so."

Joanes waited for the man to go on, but he didn't elaborate. He got back into the car.

"Shall we turn around?" asked the professor.

"It's impossible here. We'll have to go on a bit further."

Twenty minutes later, they'd only advanced about half a mile. Once again, Joanes asked which way it was to

Valladolid. Another Mexican man pointed in the opposite direction as the last guy.

Joanes took stock of the situation. At this rate, they'd take hours to get to Valladolid, where they'd still have to find accommodations for the professor and his wife. And then there was the telephone issue. The moment the wind picked up along the coast, the Federal Electricity Commission would cut the supply across the hurricane zone. They did this to prevent even more damage in the event the bad weather knocked down the overhead cables. The blackout could last for a number of days. Joanes estimated that they had about two or three hours left before the winds hit. He needed to get his phone charged before then.

"We can't stay here," the professor's wife protested. "My back is in ruins."

"Are you pretty sure it's only forty miles to Valladolid?" Joanes asked the professor.

"It could be farther. But not much. What are you thinking?"

A few feet ahead of them there was a sign marking an exit in the direction of a town three miles away—Los Tigres. There was another sign fixed to the post with wire, a rectangle of plywood painted with the words THE ENGLISH RESIDENCE. ROOMS FOR RENT.

"What do you think?" asked Joanes.

"About staying there?" the others replied together, clearly alarmed.

He relayed to them what his wife had said about the accommodation problems in Valladolid. He told them that, at this stage in the game, even if they did accept them in some hotel, they'd have no choice but to sleep on a mat in a hallway.

On hearing this, the professor's wife let out a groan.

"And what you're suggesting as an alternative," said the professor, "is to stay here, in the middle of nowhere, in the middle of the hurricane zone?"

"In Valladolid they expect the hurricane will barely have any effect at all. And we're pretty close to Valladolid."

The professor nodded, more to encourage Joanes to go on than as a sign of agreement.

"We can stay here the night," Joanes went on, "until the hurricane's past, or at least the worst of it. We'll head off in the morning."

The three of them looked at the makeshift sign.

"Who knows what it'll be like," said the professor.

"The English Residence," Joanes read aloud. "The name bodes well, at least. And right now I'll settle for any room that has a bed and four walls. And I imagine you both would, too."

The professor turned to his wife.

"What do you think?"

"I'm exhausted."

"Can't you go on a little longer?"

"A little longer?" she asked. "A little longer? How long? Haven't you heard a word of what he's been saying? We might not even have anywhere to sleep in that other place you're taking me, wherever it is."

"OK, calm down," he told his wife.

And turning back to Joanes, he said, "We don't know if they have any rooms free."

"If they don't, we'll ask for directions to Valladolid."

Joanes's grades ranged from good to excellent in all his subjects. His final undergraduate project was titled "Logical Data Modeling and Programmable Logic Controllers for Matrix Transfer and Injection Molding." Thanks to one of his professors, his meticulous work fell into the hands of a company working with industrial automata, an English multinational called Robot Systems. He was invited to interview for the Spanish branch. When the day came, a company car picked him up at his house. An English engineer wearing a shirt that matched his blue eyes gave him a tour of the most impressive part of the facility, the area where they assembled the automata's articulated arms. Finally, his guide asked him about his plans for the future and, just as Joanes had trusted would happen, asked if he would like to work there after graduation. He told him he'd be delighted, exactly as he'd practiced saying in the mirror the night before.

There was no contract or agreement of any kind, but Joanes and his wife, who by then were already a couple, celebrated as if there were. She had completed her studies in philosophy and begun giving classes as an assistant teacher in the same department, which she planned to stay in. The offer from Robot Systems tied up both of their futures.

At that point they still hadn't spoken about marriage, but they both knew they'd tie the knot sooner or later. Joanes let himself fantasize about how things might be in a couple of years. He hoped that by then he'd have already climbed up a few rungs of the ladder at Robot Systems and that he and his wife would have a couple of children. He thought, too, about buying his dad the handsome, thirty-three-foot yacht he'd been hankering after for years but had never made up his mind to buy.

Despite not having told his classmates, it didn't take long for the news of his new contract to get around the university. Robot Systems was an important company, and Joanes was heartily congratulated. Of course, there was little more than envy behind lots of the kind words; Joanes knew this and couldn't help but feel pleased with himself.

On graduation day, which took place in a soulless assembly hall with most of the light bulbs blown out and damp patches on the ceiling, he received a piece of mail with the School of Engineering letterhead on it. He guessed it was just some administrative notification, but when he tore open the envelope, he found a note written in fine, spiky handwriting. The professor had heard that Joanes would soon be starting work with Robot Systems, and he wanted to congratulate him in person and have a word with him. To that end, he invited Joanes to visit him at his home the following Saturday, at noon. He signed off with his address and requested punctuality.

The letter didn't, however, request any kind of R.S.V.P. from Joanes; the professor took it for granted that he would come when called.

Joanes kept the invitation quiet. That way he wouldn't have to answer any awkward questions when he came home. He memorized the address and threw the letter in the trash. You never knew quite what to expect from the professor.

He spent the days in the run-up to their Saturday meeting wracked with nerves and deliberating what to wear and whether he should bring a gift. He'd barely thought about the professor since passing his class. The curiosity he'd once inspired in Joanes had become buried under a sea of other day-to-day concerns and new relationships. But ever since the professor had sent him the note, he'd become a bag of nerves, jumping at the slightest touch.

He decided to see their get-together as an opportunity to talk about his studies, just like many meetings he'd had with other professors. Even so, his girlfriend noted how tense he was and asked him more than once if he was all right. He told her he was fine, but she didn't believe him. The last time she asked, on Friday evening, he snapped at her. She'd walked out of the bar without even saying goodbye.

On Saturday, at two minutes to twelve, Joanes rang the doorbell of a large house near the waterfront. He'd dressed in slacks and a shirt he'd rolled up to his elbows to give the look a laid-back air. In the end, he'd decided not to take a gift.

An old lady dressed in housekeeping attire opened the door. He introduced himself, and she asked him to follow her. She led him through an elaborately decorated lounge out onto a balcony that overlooked the sea. On the way there, Joanes caught a glimpse of the stairs that led up to the second floor. Attached to the banister was a stair lift painted the same color as the walls in an obvious effort to have it blend in with the décor. Out on the balcony, on a wrought-iron table, there were two place settings for coffee, the cups placed upside down. The housekeeper asked him to wait there.

He passed the time looking out at the view. A bank of dunes and a beach divided the house from the sea. Gusts of wind whipped up the sand and sent plastic bags and bits of paper somersaulting through the air. The balcony floor was covered in a carpet of dirty-looking sand. A heavy, salty fog, cold and hostile, drifted in off the sea. Joanes thought that he'd rather take his coffee, or whatever it was they were going to offer him, inside.

"Good morning."

He turned around, surprised, and came face to face with the professor, who was standing right behind him. He hadn't heard him approaching.

"I'm so pleased you were able to make it."

"Me too."

The professor smiled widely and made a gesture for Joanes to take a seat at the table. A second later the housekeeper appeared with an espresso maker. The professor said that he'd do the honors. Joanes sat in uncomfortable silence as he served him a coffee as thick as motor oil.

"I couldn't help but hear about your triumph."

"I wouldn't call it that."

"Don't be modest. Most of your fellow students would give their right arm to be in your place."

Joanes didn't reply, a silent admission that the professor was right. It felt like something was expanding in his chest.

"Are you familiar with the company?" asked Joanes.

"A little," said the professor, in a clear show of false modesty. "They're doing interesting things. A few of my alumni have ended up there. All of them very fine. They deserve it. And I'm very pleased for them," he said.

He stared at Joanes and took a sip of coffee, making a slight sucking sound.

The professor then proceeded to tell Joanes about his own beginnings, a definite note of nostalgia in his voice. He looked out at the horizon over the dunes as he spoke. Joanes nodded from time to time, but he was so uncomfortable, he barely registered a word of what his former teacher was saying. The professor was wearing pants not dissimilar to his own, a polo shirt with the logo of a fishing club on the chest, and some huarache loafers without socks. As is often the case with people who tend to dress formally, finding him in more casual clothes came as a shock to Joanes, as if he were seeing him in some sort of costume. He was freshly shaven, and the trace of aftershave hung on him. His sagging jowls quivered each time he laughed or sighed recalling his early professional years.

"It was harder starting out in those days," he said. "The first stage was harder, and longer. Dull, to be precise. Nowadays you all want everything right away. You think you're entitled to the whole pie from the word go. You have no concept of or interest in sacrifice."

With this, the professor returned his gaze to Joanes. The thick lenses in his glasses made his eyes look bigger than they should. He flashed Joanes a little smile and said, "Don't worry. It'll all work out well for you."

And after a pause, he repeated, "Don't worry. That's the most important thing."

The next thing, he was on his feet wrapping up their meeting. He thanked Joanes again for coming and accompanied him to the door, where he said goodbye and offered him his hand. The sound of the housekeeper bustling around in the kitchen reached them, along with the fatty smell of fried liver. That was the last time that Joanes saw the professor, until fifteen years later, when he found him on the side of a Mexican highway.

Joanes got home relieved by how quickly the meeting had flown by but at the same time disappointed. He'd never have expected anything so hackneyed from the professor as a diatribe on the immaturity of the younger generations.

He decided that their meeting wasn't worth bringing up with anyone and never said a word about it. That night he took his girlfriend out for dinner. He apologized for his behavior over the last few days. She forgave him without giving him a hard time.

First thing the following Monday morning, Joanes received a call from Robot Systems. Someone from HR let him know that the company had undergone some restructuring and that the post that he was going to fill no longer existed. The employee apologized profusely, wished him luck, and hung up.

Joanes was speechless. It took him a good several moments to hang up the telephone.

When at last he was able to think clearly again, he blamed the professor. It was clear as day—the professor had called the company to advise them against employing him. The professor was a well-known, prestigious figure whose opinion was respected, there was no doubt about it. He had clearly played down his links to Robot Systems during their meeting on Saturday. The restructuring story was, of course, a load of bull.

What he couldn't see so clearly was why the professor would do such a thing, what he'd seen in Joanes—or what he hadn't seen—in the little time they'd spent together that would lead him to give a negative report of Joanes.

But he couldn't prove anything. He couldn't even know for sure that it had really happened as he was imagining it.

And yet he knew. The cause-and-effect relationship was crystal clear to him.

The idea of paying a visit to the professor and putting him on the spot occurred to him, but it dissolved as rapidly as it had appeared. In the same way that he knew the professor was guilty, he also knew that he would deny any and all charges flatly, feigning offense.

He spent a few days taking the news in before sharing it with his family and girlfriend. He stuck to the version about the company restructuring. They were understanding and shared his disappointment, but they also assured him that there was no need to worry. He'd find something similar, if not better, in no time. He had his whole life ahead of him.

The road leading to Los Tigres wasn't as busy. It was a narrow road, riddled with bumps and potholes that looked to have been repaired countless times with tar. More homemade signs hung from the branches of trees: GOD'S GIFT TAVERN; RELIABLE ELECTRICAL PLUMBER; MECHANICAL REPAIRS BY THE GRACE OF OUR LORD JESUS ...

Los Tigres was a dump made up of low-rise houses that somehow managed to look old and at the same time only half built. The fronts of the houses were painted in gaudy colors—ochre, yellow, and lime green—but they were dirty and the paint was flaking off. Only the main road was properly paved. On first sight, its residents didn't seem to have taken any measures against the hurricane. There was an almost festive mood in the air. The streets were busy, and groups of people stood drinking outside bars.

Joanes stopped to ask for the English Residence. He was told he should go all the way to the end of town and from there keep going another third of a mile; he'd then come across a turn-off on the right. Taking that road, he'd eventually arrive at the English Residence.

Minutes later they were heading along a dirt track that led them to a two-story building painted a mustard color.

It was entirely lacking in architectural adornment and in no way distinguishable from the other houses in the town, apart from the fact that it was bigger. It, too, appeared only half built. The roof was no more than a flat surface covering the upper floor. Metal rods poked out of it, presumably the building's supports. Joanes imagined they'd stay uncut like that, just in case the owners decided to add another story. The bunches of rods, several yards high, bending under their own weight and rusting, lent the English Residence a disheveled, even lunatic appearance.

The buzzy mood in the town extended to the hotel, too. The front yard—an unpaved area of earth in front of the house—was a hive of people and vehicles. A kid directing traffic pointed to where they should leave the car.

Everyone there was Mexican. When Joanes, the professor, and his wife showed up, conversations stopped and all eyes fell on them.

"Good afternoon," said Joanes as he got out of the car. And he repeated his greeting in different directions, turning to each of the various huddles of people.

They responded with nods and murmurs.

The professor also got out. His wife stayed in the car.

One of the Mexican men was slaving away at a barbecue constructed out of a metal gas drum cut in half lengthways and mounted on sawhorses. On seeing them, he walked toward the newcomers, wiping his hands with a cloth. Joanes guessed the man was about fifty. He was built like a barrel and had one lame leg. His right foot swung, tracing an arc as he walked, and this movement drew attention to his sneakers, which had air vents snipped into the instep.

"Afternoon," said the Mexican man, introducing himself as the hotel's owner, "How can I help you?"

The professor piped up before Joanes could get a word in.

"My wife and I had a setback on the bus that was taking us to Valladolid, and we had to get off halfway through our journey. We were forced to," he clarified. "Now we're looking for accommodations for the night. In Los Tigres, they directed us this way. But before I say more, may I have a glass of water?"

The owner of the establishment went over to a table where a group of women were preparing platters of food and returned with two glasses of water.

"I'm sorry, we're out of ice."

The professor took the glasses and lifted them up to the light.

"Is it mineral water?"

"I'm sorry?"

"Is it purified?"

The Mexican man nodded unconvincingly. The professor threw him a disapproving look and went over to his wife, who drank holding the glass with both hands and spilling part of its contents down her chin. The professor stood beside her, stroking her hair. Once she'd finished, the professor offered her the other glass, which she also gulped down. Then the professor whispered something to her, to which she nodded, once again with a pained expression. Finally, the professor went up to the table of food, where he helped himself to more water and drank.

"Do you have any rooms?" Joanes asked the hotel owner.

"You're in luck. I have one. The last one. Do want to see it?"

"Just one?"

The hotel owner nodded and pointed toward the elderly couple.

"Are they your parents?"

"God no."

The professor walked back over to them, and Joanes gave him the bad news.

"It wouldn't be possible, for example, to relocate someone?" the professor proposed. "I'm sure we could come to some sort of arrangement."

"I've got people crammed in like sardines," the hotel owner answered. "Six or seven to a room. I'm not going to move them just to make more room for you."

"Is there room in any of the other hotels in Los Tigres?" interrupted Joanes.

"There aren't any other hotels in Los Tigres. Do you want to see the room?"

"We may as well, now that we're here," Joanes said.

The owner called over a vacant looking girl who was seasoning the meat for the barbecue.

"My daughter. She'll show you the room. I have to attend to the food. If you're happy with what you see, come back down and we can talk."

The professor told his wife to wait for them a minute, and he and Joanes followed the girl. Inside there was nothing vaguely resembling a reception desk. In fact, there was nothing really resembling a hotel. And this impression was heightened when they stopped in front of a room with no number on the door. The girl opened it and invited them to go in.

It was pretty large, and reasonably clean. The floor was tiled and the walls painted a muted tone of green. By way of furniture there was a bed, and next to that a bedside table with a lamp, then one sole chair set aside in the corner. A print of the Virgin of Guadalupe hung over the bed. The window faced out onto the back of the hotel, where a rusty swing set stood among weeds and garbage.

When Joanes asked if there was any chance of having an additional bed, the girl said that they could hang a hammock and pointed to some meat hooks screwed into the ceiling for that purpose.

"The bathroom is next to the kitchen," she added.

"Just one for the whole hotel?"

"There are two," answered the girl, monotone. "A ladies' room and a men's room. There are two showers, too."

Joanes flicked the lamp switch, but it didn't go on.

"There's no light," he said.

"It's been cut," said the girl. "For the hurricane."

"Already?"

"Yeah, a while ago."

Joanes let out a sigh and then asked, "How far to Valladolid from here?"

"Fifty miles or so," said the girl. "Driving it's around an hour, but if the road's backed up . . ."

"It is."

"Impossible to say, then. Are you gonna take the room?"

She looked from one to the other, waiting for an answer.

"What do you think?" Joanes asked the professor.

"It has four walls and a door. Just what you wanted."

"It could be we just have to stay one night. We'll leave tomorrow, if the weather clears up."

"Are you here because of the hurricane?" the girl asked.

Joanes nodded.

"A load of people have come because of that. If you don't take the room now, someone else will," she said, in her usual lifeless tone, barely opening her mouth.

The professor shot her a less than kindly look.

"I have to discuss it with my wife," he said, leaving the room.

Shortly after, Joanes joined the elderly couple out by the car. They were bickering under their breath.

"Have you made up your minds?"

"I'm just explaining to my wife that the room isn't very comfortable."

"It's more comfortable than the car. And it'll seem even more so when the wind picks up. She won't be any better off in Valladolid sleeping in a hallway or a gym."

"Listen to the boy," said the wife. "He's right."

"You don't want to stay?" Joanes asked the professor.

"I don't like this place. I'd take our chances and keep going."

And after a pause, he added, "We have one vote in favor of staying and another against, so you decide."

Joanes thought how with the electricity already cut, charging his phone was no longer a reason to stay. But he was tired and hungry, and he didn't feel like heading back into that traffic jam for God only knew how long. To say nothing of the hurricane. Without them even noticing, the sky had filled with heavy, gray clouds.

"We'll bed down here till tomorrow," he said. "I think that's best."

"What about your family?" asked the professor.

"They'll be fine. I'll call them and explain what's happened."

The professor stared at him.

"So it's decided," he said. "Even though, given that we're dependent on you, the truth is our opinions count for little. We're in your hands."

"I'll talk to the owner," responded Joanes, refusing to take the bait, and he walked off, leaving the elderly couple to go on exchanging whispers.

"We'll take it."

The owner nodded, satisfied, and without taking

his eyes off the barbecue. He was putting a lot of care and attention into his work. Despite the fact that there were other men around, not one offered him their help or advice on how best to cook the meat, as one might expect.

"How much is the room?"

The owner gave his price. It was more than the room was worth, but in the current circumstances, reasonable enough.

"How long are you going to stay?"

"A night. Two, at most. Do you want payment now?"

"No, don't worry. We'll discuss that tomorrow. There's a lot of folks here," he added, waving his meat fork toward the mass. "There's no way of you slipping away without me knowing about it."

"Why is it called the English Residence?"

"An English couple lived here before. Archeologists. They came for the ruins and stayed twenty years. This was their house. When they died, it was abandoned. We tore it down and built our own on top."

"So there are no English people now."

"Not one."

"So . . . this is a hotel."

The owner looked at him as if he didn't understand.

"It's just it doesn't say anywhere that it's a hotel," Joanes explained.

"It has a lot of rooms, and I rent them out. It's a hotel."

"I see. Are they guests, too?" asked Joanes, referring to the others. There were close to forty people out on the lawn, sitting on plastic chairs under umbrellas advertising Coca-Cola.

"Only a few of them," said the owner with a resigned smile. "Almost all of them are family. They've come for shelter."

"Your relatives?"

"And my wife's. It's a tradition. When there's a hurricane, those of them who live on the coast come here to the English Residence."

"Do you think the hurricane will reach us here?"

"It'll get a bit breezy."

"Enough to worry about?"

"Only if you want to, my friend. Anyway, why don't you make yourselves comfortable and eat something?" said the owner, pointing to the meat on the barbecue. "It's *cochinita*. Like it?"

Joanes nodded.

The professor pushed his wife to the room in her wheelchair. Joanes followed them with the luggage. The professor settled his wife in the bed, refusing Joanes's help. She fell down onto the bed with a moan, whether of pleasure or pain Joanes couldn't tell.

"Are you all right like that?"

If she said anything in reply, only the professor heard her.

"I'll bring you more water and something to eat," he said. "Do you need anything else?"

"My mask," she murmured.

The professor rummaged in the travel bag until he came across her eye mask. Very carefully, he put it on his wife. Then he gestured to Joanes to leave the room and followed him out.

Once in the hallway, lowering his voice, Joanes asked the professor if his wife was all right.

"Yes, of course she is. She's just tired and . . . well, the whole commotion on the bus took its toll on her. But that's understandable, wouldn't you say?"

Once he'd freshened up, having waited a long time in line for the restroom, Joanes went back outside. He kept his backpack on him, reluctant to leave it in the room. The hotel owner waved him over and dished a monumental portion of meat onto his paper plate. The other guests were already eating. Several women were tending a table filled with platters of potatoes, rice, tortillas, beans, *chiles rellenos*, plantain *tamales*, and *mole* chicken.

Joanes grabbed a chair and took it over to the edge of the lawn, just where the plants and creepers that surrounded the hotel began. On his way, he picked up a beer from a tub of water with cans of drinks floating inside.

He ought to call his family before eating. He imagined them in their room in the evacuation hotel. His father-in-law would be spouting nonsense and praising his new bride's latest stroke of genius. His daughter, her hair falling over her face as a kind of barrier against the adults, would be curled up in a corner working on the nihilistic vampire novel she'd been writing for months. And as for his wife, Joanes imagined her checking her watch and asking herself where in the hell he'd gotten to.

He looked at the battery icon on his cell phone. It would have to be a quick conversation. He needed the rest of the battery to sort out the hotel offer with his client. He dialed the number of the evacuation hotel and asked to be put through to his family's room. The phone rang three times, four . . .

"Come on, come on . . . where are you?"

On the sixth ring, he hung up and dialed the number again. He left a message for his wife, explaining what had happened and that he would get to Valladolid the following day. He added that it was important she didn't call him, so he could save his battery.

"Did you get all that?"

"Yes, sir," answered the employee at the other end of the line. "I'll be sure to pass it on to your wife."

But Joanes wasn't convinced. He could hear a lot going on in the background, a real racket, and it seemed to him that the hotel employee had more pressing things to attend to than taking down his message. But he couldn't waste any more time repeating himself. He hung up without saying goodbye and looked again at the battery icon on the screen. He put the phone away in his backpack and nibbled on his *cochinita*. More than a few of the Mexican folks sat brazenly staring at him. He felt utterly depressed all of a sudden. He wanted to say to hell with it all and talk to his wife until he'd used up every last drop of battery. Hearing her voice always calmed him down. She would almost certainly have some sound piece of advice for him.

He saw the professor coming out of the hotel. He'd put on a clean shirt. Joanes watched him as he chose from the platters of food and served out small portions of everything on two plates, but so that no one food type touched another. Afterward, the professor made one of the Mexican women attending the table bring him a tray so he could take the plates up to the room. He didn't notice Joanes, or if he did, he didn't bother to say hello.

Joanes polished off his food and grabbed another beer, not caring that it was warm. He felt a bit better with a full stomach. A band of children paraded one after the other in front of him, some stopping to stare at him. He made faces at them, but they weren't laughing. Little by little, the lawn was emptying; as soon as people finished eating, they looked up at the sky and retreated to their rooms. The women looking after the table had begun taking in the food. One of them came out of the hotel with a palm frond and began to sweep the dirt yard, which made the others laugh. The wind would take care of that.

He was exhausted but stayed outside. He didn't want to go back to the room while the professor and his wife were eating. He waited with his elbows resting on his knees and his chin on his fists, not paying any attention to the kids that circled around him, staring as if he were some weirdo.

He wondered what the professor and his wife might be up to. Perhaps they'd fallen asleep. After a little while, he told himself there was no reason to keep waiting; after all, the room was partly his, too. But just as he was about to get to his feet, he saw the professor coming out of the hotel. The don looked around, spotted Joanes, and walked straight over to him.

"Do you have a telephone? I need to make an urgent call to Egypt."

Joanes stood up. He stared at him before answering.

"I'm sorry, my phone is out of battery. I used it up talking to my wife."

The professor tutted.

"Well! That is very bad news indeed. You can't imagine how bad."

"I'm sorry," repeated Joanes. "Can I ask why exactly you need to call Egypt?"

"My son's been in an accident. He was deep sea diving in the Red Sea, and something went wrong. I don't know the details."

The professor pressed his lips closed, composing himself.

"It happened yesterday, but we didn't find out until this morning. They called us at the hotel, just before we got on the bus."

"Where were you staying?"

"In Cancún. We came to Mexico for a conference I had to give in Mexico City. That was last week. My wife insisted that we take a few days' vacation in the Caribbean afterward."

"Is your son very bad?" Joanes asked gingerly.

The professor shrugged with his palms facing up in a gesture of helplessness.

"I don't know. I only had a second to talk to his partner, and the doctors still hadn't said anything at that point. Later, from the bus, I was able to get through, but they couldn't tell me anything other than that my son was under observation, no change. By the looks of things, we'll just have to sit and wait."

There was a pause, after which he added, "I have to find out how he is."

"Of course," muttered Joanes. "You say you tried to call from the bus; so you have a telephone, then."

"I had one. But I lost it. There was . . . how can I put it? There was a ruckus when they threw us off the bus, and I lost my phone. It must have fallen out of my pocket. I only realized after the bus had already driven off."

"Seems like it's been a rough day for you two."

The professor agreed wordlessly.

"And it will continue to be for as long as we don't know what's happened to our son."

"Perhaps someone could lend you a phone."

The professor shook his head.

"I've asked several people. They say the electricity is cut and that if their battery runs out, they'll have no way of recharging it. And no one knows how long it'll take for the electricity supply to return, so everyone's keeping their phones to themselves."

"Perhaps with a little financial incentive . . ."

"I've tried, but it's no use. And the hotel doesn't have a land line."

"You could offer more."

"They've told me not to ask again."

And lowering his voice, the professor added, "Some of them got a bit aggressive. They say that the system's overloaded and that even if I tried, I wouldn't be able to get through and I'd just be wasting their battery."

There was a pause before he added, "I don't think these people have taken much of a shine to me. It's a good thing we're with you. Although it's a shame your phone is no use."

He said all this looking hard at Joanes, who averted his gaze and began staring at the weeds growing beyond the yard. The professor knew that expression well, it was the same one his students pulled when he threatened them with a question—a mixture of fear and shame.

"It's a pity you didn't ask to borrow my phone earlier, when you could have used it."

"Yes, a pity. But I prefer to work my own problems out wherever possible."

"Maybe the lines will come back later and someone will lend you their phone. My advice to you is to keep asking," said Joanes.

"Yes, maybe," was the professor's laconic response.

"And now, if it's all right with you, I'd like to go up to the room and get a little rest."

"Of course. It's your room, too. Give me a minute or two to see how my wife is. Then come up whenever you like."

Joanes needed a minute to go over what had just happened. He unzipped his backpack and checked the phone battery again. It was nighttime in Spain. There was almost no

78

chance he'd receive the call he was waiting for in the next several hours. But it could well come tomorrow. He had to save his battery.

As for the professor, he could use any old phone so long as it could make international calls. And there had to be a load of them in the hotel. As long as he used a bit of tact, someone would likely end up lending him one. If there was one thing Joanes was sure of, it was the professor's powers of persuasion.

What's more, he wasn't absolutely convinced that it was an emergency. The professor knew only that his son had been in an accident. Not whether or not he was seriously injured. And in any case, even if he did manage to make contact with the hospital or whatever place his son was in, how would that change anything? It wouldn't make his son any better. At most, the call might put the professor and his wife's minds at rest—if the news was good. Joanes preferred not to think about what would happen if the opposite were the case, if the news didn't bode well or was out and out bad. He couldn't bring himself to imagine what it would be like to be locked up for hours, days even, with an elderly couple who'd just lost their son.

But for the time being, he went on reasoning with himself, making the call simply wasn't an option, so they'd have to put up with the lack of information. He had brought them this far, at least. And arranged them a place to stay for the night. That was all he could do for the time being.

He defended his decision by telling himself that he truly *needed* the phone.

He tried to imagine what his wife and daughter would think if they were there. His wife would question his decision at first, but her practical side would take over and in the end she'd side with Joanes. His daughter would say that he was despicable, making her feelings absolutely clear to him. And yet, for better or for worse, neither of them was there.

He was snapped out of his thoughts by a sudden gust of wind, so strong it nearly knocked him to the ground. The trees rustled. and even the metal rods sticking out of the roof of the English Residence made a gentle clinking sound. The gust barely lasted a few seconds and was followed by a cool, blustery breeze that also disappeared a moment later. Joanes and the few Mexican guests that remained outside looked up to the clouds, clearly anxious; that had been no more than a taste of what was to come. Calm was restored to the yard, but this did little to reassure the people still out there, who began edging towards the hotel.

On the east coast of Yucatán, the wind had already begun to blow with some force. A salty rain would follow it—ocean water, picked up and dragged along by the hurricane, accompanied by gulfweed and corral and fish, some of which would still be alive, flapping around on roads and backyard patios, on the roofs of houses and in the jungle, among the dark roots of trees many miles inland.

Three months after his visit to the professor's house, Joanes started working in a modestly sized company that made telephone cables. A year later, he and his girlfriend got married, and almost immediately after that, she became pregnant.

Joanes tried to do his best at work, but things didn't go as well as he or his superiors hoped they would. He felt out of place there, and pined for the post that never was at Robot Systems. He realized that he'd wanted it much more than he'd previously realized. He ended up convincing himself he'd been destined for that job and that now that it was out of his grasp, no other job would ever be right for him. Time and again, his initiatives at the company came to nothing.

After a couple of years, he was transferred to a secondary department whose main role was replacing the polyethylene covers on cables. His performance there also stood out for all the wrong reasons.

One evening, on his way home, he heard someone calling his name as he sat in a line of cars all waiting to reach the tollbooth. In the adjacent line, a driver was waving his arm, trying to catch Joanes's attention, half his body hanging out of the car window. It turned out to be an old friend from the School of Engineering. They hadn't seen each other since graduation. Yelling from car to car, they agreed to meet up in town for a few beers.

Things weren't going so bad for his friend. He headed up a small air conditioning firm, where he acted as an intermediary between manufacturers and clients, and at the moment he found himself with more work than he could manage alone. He dropped into the conversation that it wouldn't be a bad idea for him to have a partner with some technical know-how. Joanes didn't take the hint, but that night he told his wife about it. It was true that he'd never seen himself at the helm of an air conditioning company, but the opportunity had come up at just the right moment, and it was pretty tempting—just two partners, no one above him, the chance to make decisions . . .

As part of joining the company, he was required to invest some capital, capital he didn't have. He spoke to his father, who gave him the money he'd been saving for his yacht. Joanes promised to repay him the moment he could.

For a while things went swimmingly, exactly as Joanes had hoped, and better. The business grew. He repaid his father the money he'd borrowed—although his father still didn't buy himself the boat. And Joanes, his wife, and his daughter left the apartment they'd moved into after the wedding and rented a bigger one. Even then they didn't imagine staying there forever. They began saving up to buy a house—one with a sea view.

But as the years went by, his friend became more and more distrustful and distant. He avoided Joanes outside work hours. He assigned himself all the business trips, as if he wanted to spend as little time as possible in the office. Things went on like this until, one day, he revealed his plan to up sticks and move to a bigger city. He offered his part of the business to Joanes, who could either take it over entirely or risk someone else buying it, someone he might not get along with as well. He talked it through with his wife, and the two of them together opted for the former. They dipped into their house savings, and Joanes, once again, asked his dad for help.

Suddenly he owned one hundred percent of the business.

And then things took a turn for the worse. The jobs began to dry up, as if his ex-partner had been the only one the clients trusted. The formerly profitable business was being run into the ground, and in a matter of months it was on the cusp of insolvency. Joanes began to think that perhaps he'd had nothing to do with its previous success, that it had all been thanks to his ex-partner. Now that he, and he alone, was at the helm, the whole thing was falling apart. None of his efforts came to anything, just as had happened at the telephone cable company.

Over all those years, he'd never forgotten his visit to see the professor, but when the company began to go from bad to worse, the memory came back on a daily basis to haunt him. He no longer wondered what the professor had seen in him to discourage his hiring at Robot Systems; the problem was perfectly clear from the way everything had gone for him since. Now he asked himself how the professor had managed to see it, how he'd come by his power of prescience. And he asked himself, too, if during the little time that they'd spent there on that balcony, from the few words that they'd exchanged, the professor had perceived anything more than a bleak professional future.

The nights he couldn't sleep, when all those thoughts came into his head, spinning in an endless spiral, his self-respect kicked in as a kind of defense mechanism.

Accurate as the professor's intuition might have been, it didn't allow him to see into the future. If he hadn't recommended Joanes for Robot Systems, perhaps it was because he wanted the post for some family member or friend, or perhaps for an even more banal reason, like, for instance, him not liking some physical feature of Joanes's or because of the geographical implications of his last name.

But not even this idea offered him any relief, because beyond any of the possible reasons the professor might have had at the time, Joanes, and Joanes alone, was responsible for his pitiful career.

And a second later he'd tell himself no, that he couldn't be the only one responsible. That there must be someone else to blame, someone to share some of the responsibility. And his old don fitted the bill just perfectly.

And in this way the professor became the virtual stooge for Joanes's problems. During their brief encounter on the balcony, he hadn't merely foreseen the unfortunate future that lay in store for the boy who'd once been his student; he—the professor—had provoked it. For whatever reason, he had condemned him in some way, cursed him.

Joanes let himself think this way. And in time he came to believe it. The professor became a vessel for all his frustrations and rage. And the vessel gradually filled up, and its contents grew more and more viscous, until eventually they became as hard as stone; the professor was no longer a mere emotional device, a fantasy for self-exoneration, he'd become the one true culprit of everything bad that had ever happened to Joanes.

The room measured four by five feet. While it had seemed big enough at first, now it gave Joanes the impression that there was barely space to move. He stood waiting, unsure what to do. The professor was sitting in the only available seat, which he'd put next to the bed where his wife was resting. She'd changed into a pale pink dress, as much like a hospital gown as the previous one. She looked a little better. Her husband had helped her freshen up. On the floor there was a washbowl with soapy water and a sponge inside. The professor had also gotten ahold of a pillow, and his wife was resting, her head upright, against it.

"That strange girl, the owner's daughter, came by," said the professor. "She put the hammock up."

Joanes would have more than happily thrown himself into the hammock, but he rejected the idea; the stance would have seemed too indolent, insulting even, given the circumstances. Instead of lying down, he went over to the window and remained there, on his feet. Apart from the chair where the professor was sitting, there was just one other seat—the wheelchair. He didn't even entertain the idea.

"How are you doing?" he asked the woman.

She cocked her head in a gesture that could have meant anything.

The professor was holding a damp handkerchief, which every now and then he used to cool her forehead. His face betrayed no emotion whatsoever. He wore the same vacant expression he used to in class when he would fall suddenly into one of his absorbed silences. If someone had asked Joanes what the professor might be feeling, he'd have said "exhaustion" or "anger" long before "concern."

A few minutes later, his wife began to make fitful snoring sounds, and the professor got to his feet, taking care not to wake her. He moved over to the window. Joanes and he both looked out.

Up in the sky, the black silhouettes of a few vast birds traced out circles around a single point in the undergrowth.

"There's something out there in agony, or something dying," said the professor, almost in a whisper. "Did you know that in ancient Egypt it was a commonly held belief that there were no male buzzards, only females? And that when the time came to reproduce, these females would simply expose their vaginas to the wind?"

After a meditative pause he added, "It's not a bad method. Pretty agreeable, if you ask me. Avoids unnecessary ties."

Joanes considered this affected, erudite, and ultimately useless statement as the kind of thing the professor would come out with when he wanted to assert his superiority over the students.

"They're not buzzards, they're black vultures," he said.

"Isn't that the same thing?"

"I believe not."

The professor watched the birds keenly, squinting his eyes.

"Buzzards, black vultures . . . it's all the same."

He went on, "You're lucky your family isn't here."

86

Joanes conceded the point.

"I'm glad they don't have to spend the night in this place," he said.

"That's not what I mean. I mean that *you're* lucky. You're not dependent on anybody, and nobody's dependent on you."

Joanes nodded in agreement. Then he said, "You're right."

"Are your wife and daughter alone?"

"No. My father-in-law's with them."

"Even more reason to feel lucky. He'll look after them."

Joanes imagined his wife and daughter under the care of his father-in-law and felt a mixture of relief and remorse. It also occurred to him in that same moment how alike the professor and his father-in-law were, in various ways.

"I'm going to keep hunting for a telephone," said the professor. "In all likelihood, the wind will blow some telephone tower down soon, and then I'll have no way of calling. Would you mind staying with her?" he asked, gesturing toward his wife.

"Of course not."

The professor left the door ajar on his way out, to let some air into the stifling room. A couple of kids were chasing each other up and down the hallway. Every time they passed the room, they would stop and look inside, grinning. When they appeared for the umpteenth time, the professor's wife opened her eyes and, in a reedy whisper, asked Joanes if he could close the door. He did as she asked.

"Where is he?"

"Your husband? He's gone to look for a telephone."

She tried to sit up, and Joanes helped her, arranging the pillow she was leaning against.

"You're very gentlemanly."

"It's nothing."

"You've been very kind to us, and I still haven't thanked you."

"Forget about it. I wish I could have gotten you to Valladolid. And I wish you had a better place to get some rest."

Despite having closed the door, the hotel noises could be clearly heard. Footsteps, voices, laughter. Doors were repeatedly being slammed.

She closed her eyes and pinched the bridge of her nose.

"Don't you wish there were some kind of gadget that could give us absolute silence? Headphones, or something like that. Something connected to a container filled with silence."

"It already exists," said Joanes. "They're called earplugs."

The professor's wife shook her head.

"You misunderstand. I'm not talking about preventing sounds from entering you, but rather *introducing* silence into your body. Having it fill up your lungs, course through your veins."

It seemed to Joanes that the most appropriate response to a statement like that was to keep his mouth shut. She stared at him intensely.

"You were a student of my husband's."

Joanes nodded.

"Did he make your life miserable?"

"No."

The speed with which he answered made her smile.

"You're too polite. Come on, you can tell me. I won't tell him. He fucked up your life?"

Joanes was silent.

"Of course he did," she continued. "He loved doing that. Fucking with his students. And even those who weren't his students. He liked that, too."

Joanes didn't respond.

"Come on," she insisted. "He made things really hard? You still have nightmares about him? I know that lots of you do. Even I have them."

"No," answered Joanes. "He didn't fuck with me more than anyone else."

"Well, that makes you one of the lucky ones, I can assure you."

She groped around on the bed for her eye mask, like a blind person, and put it on, her hands shaking. Then she sighed and went still.

With the door closed, the heat was even more intense. Joanes felt the sweat dripping down between his shoulder blades. He tried to open the window, taking advantage of the breeze before the wind became too stormy, but as he wrestled with the handle, the professor's wife told him to let it be. She'd lifted one end of the mask and was looking at him out of one eye.

"If you open it, the mosquitoes will get in. They're worse than the heat."

"I think I have some repellent in my first aid kit."

"It smells terrible. Makes me dizzy."

And with that, she pulled down her eye mask, concluding the conversation.

The professor was back before long.

"Did you get ahold of a phone?" asked Joanes.

"Yes, in exchange for every last dime I had on me. But given the circumstances, I wasn't about to start haggling."

"Any luck?"

The professor shook his head.

"They were right—the lines are down. I tried three times."

Over on the bed, his wife, who had taken off her eye mask on hearing him enter the room, turned and looked over at the window.

"I'm sorry," said Joanes. "Maybe you'll have more luck later."

"I can't imagine how," muttered the professor, taking a seat.

But he wouldn't be defeated. That wasn't his style. He straightened up, took a deep breath, and in a split second was back to his normal self.

"No doubt you're regretting having stopped to bury that monkey now. If you hadn't done that, you'd be with your family in a real hotel by now. Not putting up with our rotten company."

"I did what I thought was right at the time."

"And do you still feel the same?"

Joanes looked around their sad little hotel room—its badly aligned walls full of cracks that had been filled in with plaster, the faded print of the Virgin of Guadalupe hanging above the bed.

"Yes," he said firmly. "I'd do the same again."

"Interesting," said the professor.

Joanes thought it best to change the subject.

"What was your conference about?" he asked.

"I'm sorry?"

"The conference you came to give in Mexico City."

The professor thought for a second, as if trying to remember something that had happened years ago, not the week before.

"It was called 'Ethical Considerations On Artificial Intelligence.'"

"Sounds interesting."

"It is," the professor answered categorically.

"Would you tell me a little bit about it?"

90

"I don't think now is the time."

"Why not? It's not like we have anything else to do."

The professor thought about it for a second then nodded, clearly unconvinced. He began with a kind of telegraphic listing off of the main points of the conference, but the more he went on, the more he seemed to settle into his own words, as if they filled him with confidence, and his speech became increasingly exhaustive. He talked about the possibilities and risks involved in creating a machine that might "think too much," about whether the process of building a thinking machine qualifies as a form of reproduction, whether that machine should therefore be considered "natural" or "unnatural," and about the ethical implications of each and every one of these cases.

Joanes had sat down on the floor, his back against the wall. With him in this position, and the professor sitting in the chair, it was as if he were being given a lecture, something that neither of them failed to notice.

Once the professor finished his overview, they went on discussing the matter in more detail, keeping their voices down so as not to disturb the professor's wife. Joanes was feeling more and more at ease. He was enjoying their sophisticated tête-à-tête, such a welcome change from the mind-numbing and intellectually undemanding discussions over costs and energy efficiency that he had in his day job. He hadn't felt that animated for ages, and he had the impression that the professor, too, was enjoying himself. The conversation acted as a bubble that isolated and protected them from their surroundings, shutting out the woeful hotel, the hurricane, and all their worries. The professor even seemed to have forgotten about his son's accident. With nothing but words, they'd created an intellectual environment, a warm microclimate of contemplation familiar to them both and in which they felt safe and sure of themselves.

The conversation grew livelier by the minute, and not even an intermission when the professor had to help his wife to the bathroom diminished their satisfaction at the moment.

"The conference was, on the whole, an extremely agreeable experience," the professor explained as he returned to the room. "It was a shame that in the Q & A session someone had to lower the tone."

"What happened?" asked Joanes.

"An audience member, someone with a clear antagonistic streak, explained what he thought would happen if further developments in the field of AI led to the creation of a intelligence surpassing that of human beings. *As he saw it*, such an intelligence would prompt a new moral order, one based on the machines and more elevated than man's. He suggested that such a moral order might well represent the origin of a new religion."

"What did you answer?" asked Joanes after an expectant pause.

"I spoke to him about Hans Hörbiger and his World Ice Doctrine."

"I'm sorry, I'm afraid I don't know who he is."

The professor nodded and cleared his throat before speaking again.

"Hans Hörbiger was born in Austria in the middle of the nineteenth century. He studied engineering and specialized in steam-powered machinery and compressors. He invented an incredibly low-friction valve, patented it, and before he knew it was a millionaire. He created a company to commercialize his invention and left it in the hands of his son. From that day on, he dedicated himself wholly to *scientific investigation*."

"Our friend Hörbiger had two passions. The first was astronomy, and the second, as it is for most experts in steam-powered machinery, the transformation of water into its various states. From his telescopic observations, he had begun to suspect that the reflections he saw on the Moon were produced by great masses of ice, which in turn led him to think that the entire satellite was formed of this substance. What's more, he believed that the same was true of other celestial bodies. Most likely he had this idea in mind when, one winter's day, on a visit to a steelworks, he noticed how a quantity of molten steel spilled over the frozen ground. The earth sizzled and spat and cracked open under the burning steel and produced violent explosions of steam. Hörbiger had an epiphany."

"The entire universe had to be the result of a encounter between ice and fire. Hörbiger imagined the origin of the universe as a collision between an enormous, incandescent mass—a super sun—and another mass of immense proportions, in this case made of ice. The meeting of these two bodies provoked a colossal explosion that broke both into pieces, which were then scattered throughout space. Out of this came fragments made solely of ice, like the Moon, others made solely of fire, like the Sun, and others, like Earth, made out of a combination of the two. Are you still with me?"

Joanes nodded a yes.

"Next, Hörbiger concluded his cosmogony by applying to it the Law of Universal Gravitation, or an adapted version of it. According to him, astral bodies did not adhere to fixed orbits around the larger bodies, as the Moon does around us. He believed that forces of attraction possessed a greater power than repulsive forces. As a result, a satellite, like the Moon, would not trace an elliptical orbit around its planet but rather a slow spiral that would gradually draw it toward the planet. At the end of this spiral, the two bodies would collide in a new cataclysm of fire and ice. According to Hörbiger, this will have happened various times since the beginning of the universe. Our Moon must be the fourth to have circled us since the beginning of time. Three others would have preceded it, each with their own resulting cataclysm."

The professor paused for a moment and cleared his throat before going on.

"Up to this point, Hörbiger's theory, however erroneous, is based on scientific principles and would merit at least some consideration. But notes of fantasy-science gradually begin to creep in. The Moon's approach toward the Earth, he suggested, must be very slow, which means there must also be a lengthy period—of several thousands of years—in which the two bodies find themselves in very close proximity. In this interval, the combined gravitational pulls of the satellite and the planet would have certain effects on the Earth's inhabitants, primarily on their size. In other words, it would have been an age of giants. The Earth would have been populated by plants, animals, and human beings, all giant."

"These giants wouldn't have been entirely wiped from the Earth during the final collision. Some of them, the fittest, the super-giants, would have survived, and from there life on Earth would have regenerated. As you can see, a load of baloney."

"But this boloney fell on fertile ground; ground peopled by goosestep aficionados and Wagner-loving opera-goers. Hörbiger's cosmology fitted the burgeoning national socialist mythology like a glove. All those tales of giants, cataclysms, frozen landscapes, and biologically privileged survivors resounded perfectly with the Nordic mythology so admired by the Führer. Hitler adopted Hörbiger's hypotheses as his own. As such, the deliriums of a madman who should never have left his valve workshop ended up turning into doctrine."

"But we're talking about the 1930s," interrupted Joanes, "not the Middle Ages. Those deliriums would have met with staunch opposition."

The professor threw him a pitying smile.

"Hörbiger considered objective science to be a kind of totem in decline. He also claimed that man's preoccupation with coherence is a deadly vice. And Hitler thought the same. What's more, as well you know, the Nazis' methods for silencing their opposition were as effective as they were uncivilized."

"I don't see the relevance of this to your argument," said Joanes. "The dramatic or truly problematic element of this story isn't that a mystic or religious doctrine was extrapolated from a scientific discovery, but the fact that this doctrine was espoused by another, larger one for exclusively utilitarian motives. The Nazis appropriated Hörbiger's cosmogony not because they really believed in it, but because it suited their interests. The truly despicable thing is to carry an ideology, in this case National Socialism, to such twisted extremes."

"I'm not sure that the Nazis didn't believe in The World Ice Doctrine," the professor responded, "although it's possible that you know more on this matter than I do. In any case, what really matters here is that his cosmogony was accepted thanks in great part to its scientific foundations, which lent it credibility. Worse still, they converted it into something applicable to the real world. Hitler believed that by simply adhering to The World Ice Doctrine, ice would obey him, as if by uncovering the secrets of ice's origin and behavior, the Führer could become its master. When he launched his winter campaign against Russia during the Second World War, Hitler spoke of how the cold was going to obey him like one of his generals. Of course, you're well aware of what really happened. Temperatures dropped to as low as forty below, liquid syngas disassociated, and vehicles stopped working, soldiers would bend down to defecate, and their asses would turn into ice donuts. Until one of Hitler's generals dared to ask him to reconsider the Russian assault. Do you know what his response was?"

Joanes did know, and hastened to answer.

"'Leave winter to me. You, attack.'"

"That's right. That was more or less Hitler's answer. And he meant it literally; he believed he could control the cold."

Joanes was still at a loss as to the relevance of the story. The reference to Nazism, what's more, seemed to him an extreme measure. To his mind, anyone who resorted to those kinds of references, even to berate them, was employing the kind of radical, devastating argument that was all too reminiscent of the National Socialists themselves. There was something premeditated, too, about the professor's argument, a hunch that only fueled Joanes's general suspicion. His whole cosmogony spiel seemed pre-rehearsed, as indicated by the—albeit shoddy—alliteration of a phrase like "the earth sizzled and spat and cracked open," and his way of introducing the Nazis as "Wagner-loving opera-goers."

Joanes imagined the professor in his study or his office or wherever it was he worked, researching and putting his speech together, reading it aloud, adjusting the story to the lesson he wanted to communicate through it. It was clear the professor had not been irritated by the interruption to his conference. Quite the contrary. He'd delighted in the opportunity to share the story with an audience, and he was so self-satisfied that now he was treating Joanes to another round.

"And there's an even more serious problem," the professor was saying. "And this is precisely what I tried to make that gentleman at the conference understand when he began speculating over whether a new religion could arise out of Artificial Intelligence. If something like that happened, as was the case with Hörbiger, we'd find ourselves with a case of regression. A scientific advance, a rational advance, a logical advance would make us move backward *of our own free will* to a state of pre-logical thinking."

He paused to let his words sink in and added, "And what's more, this regression would discredit the achievements of the logical advancement that occasioned it. We mustn't forget that Hörbiger was right, up to a point. It is true that there are celestial bodies out there composed of ice, like comets and the rings of Saturn, and it's also true that there's ice on the Moon. We must prevent such kinds of discrediting," said the professor, pointing an admonishing finger at Joanes, as if he were still his student. "We must never give in to what Jung called 'the libido of the unreasonable.'"

Joanes shifted position, and his joints cricked. The professor's wife remained unmoving on the bed, looking out into the nothingness like a zombie.

"And yet . . ." Joanes began, as if speaking to himself, but he fell silent again without adding anything.

"And yet what?" the professor prompted him.

"And yet it's natural, after all, for man to give in to 'the libido of the unreasonable.'"

"Explain yourself."

"It's a natural consequence of our thirst for knowledge. If science takes its time offering us answers, then we have to fill in the gaps with—"

"With what? With fallacies? With mythology?"

"Not always," responded Joanes. "The physical or mathematical models that scientists use perform the same function. Researchers use them to try to explain what we don't know. And that leads us to findings as incorrect as those occasioned by religious meddling and myth."

"You couldn't be more wrong. Scientific models are hypotheses based on verified facts. They're not born with the aim of surviving, as religions are, nor of reaching above or beyond themselves, as also happens with religions, rather their aim is to provide a working basis until the number of experimentally verified facts increases."

"I was only offering a point of comparison," explained Joanes. "I wasn't saying that the scientific model exists on the same level as Hörbiger's cosmogony."

"I'm pleased to hear it, bearing in mind you're one of my alumni."

Joanes wiped the sweat from his brow.

"Scientists have the necessary discipline and knowledge to keep their conjectures under control," he ventured, "but what happens when unanticipated or tricky or only partly explicable facts, which are the cause of such conjectures, move into a wider forum? In such a case, it's little wonder the hypothesis gets out of control, as happened when Hörbiger's ideas came to the Nazis' attention."

"That was an extremely specific case," said the professor.

He spoke softly, waiting to see where his old student's argument was leading.

Joanes perked up again. He could tell the professor was not enjoying having someone stand up to him.

"Of course it's a specific case," he went on, "to which we must add that Hörbiger's ideas couldn't be qualified even as a hypothesis. The World Ice Doctrine didn't have a sufficiently solid scientific basis to endure without Hitler's backing. But what would have happened if the doctrine's origins had been altogether different, unquestionably sound and at the same time attractive to a great number of people, demanding our consideration."

"You mean, for example, something like Artificial Intelligence?"

"I don't know enough about AI, although I understand why the gentleman at the conference asked what he did."

"Give me an example."

"Imagine a tesseract, a hypercube, a four dimensional cube. Do you know what that is?"

"Of course," the professor replied, glacial.

"Let's imagine, then, that a century ago, a tesseract appeared before three shepherd children herding their flock on the outskirts of Fatima. What would have happened?"

"Nothing," responded the professor, growing more and more irritated. "We live in three-dimensional space. The shepherd children would have seen nothing more than a normal, run-of-the-mill cube, not its projection in the fourth dimension."

"What I mean is let's *imagine* what would have happened if that four dimensional cube had appeared as such. I'm talking *in abstracto*."

"I understand perfectly well what you're trying to say. A separate question is whether it's a pertinent example. I happen to believe it is not."

Joanes didn't let himself be put off.

"A tesseract is inconceivable in our world," he said. "It's a theoretical *construct*, but no less real for that. Mathematicians use it every day, extend it to five dimensions, to the nth dimension, lend it practical applications. So tesseracts are real and at the same time . . . fantastical. Let's call them that. Now let's suppose that one manifested itself as it really is. What would the young shepherds have done? What would they have believed they were seeing? What conclusions would such a vision have led them to when considered in conjunction with the traditional tales or the Sunday sermons they were used to? In what way would their vision have morphed the moment they put it into words and shared it with their neighbors? Might there not exist, today, in Fatima, a shrine—one perhaps with a different image at the altar, but a shrine nonetheless—to which devotees of the fourth dimension would make their pilgrimage?"

"Enough!" exclaimed the professor.

"What I'm trying to explain to you is that—"

The professor jumped out of his chair.

"There's nothing you can explain to me!"

His face was red, and he clenched his fists as if about to punch his old student.

"OK," said Joanes, getting to his feet. "Don't get mad. I thought we were just talking, like colleagues."

"Colleagues?" asked the professor. "Colleagues? You and I?"

"OK, OK. I've got it."

"Be quiet! Not another word! Don't make things worse than they already are."

And muttering away, the professor exclaimed, "Idiot!"

Joanes swallowed hard.

"I won't hold that one against you," he said. "You're having a difficult time and—"

"Don't you dare patronize me! Who do you think you are?"

100

Joanes was looking for the words to answer when the professor's wife piped up.

"You should see yourselves," she said, rubbing her temples. "You're behaving like morons. And worse still, you're a pair of bores. Why don't you talk about something else? You and your math," she said to her husband. "You can never keep your cool when you talk about math."

"We're not talking about math exactly," he retorted.

"Change the subject," she requested.

Just then, the door to the room opened, and a soft light filtered in. The owner's daughter looked at them with her customary poker face. She was holding a bottle with a candle sticking out of it. The room was almost pitch black. The storm had brought the evening on early.

"Don't you know how to knock?" asked the professor.

"I did. You didn't hear me," said the girl.

"Sure you did," said the professor. "Is that for us?"

The girl nodded and held out the candle. The professor got up to take it and left it on the table next to the bed.

"Thank you," he said, not a hint of appreciation in his voice.

The girl backed out and closed the door without a sound.

Nobody moved or said a word for a moment, until the professor's wife repeated, "Change the subject."

"Don't you speak to me like that!" responded the professor. "If I hadn't listened to you when you wanted to stay on in Mexico, we'd be on our way to see our son already. It's your fault we're here!"

The woman's face was illuminated by the candle next to the bed. On hearing these words, she put her hands over her face, but she neither uttered a word nor made a sound. Joanes guessed she was crying, but when she moved her hands away, her eyes were dry.

"I'm sorry," she said to Joanes. "I'm very sorry. I wish you didn't have to see us in pieces like this, overcome with pain. I wish you didn't have to share this room with us. We're making things hard for you. You, who've been so kind to us. I'm sorry."

And then the tears did come, and her sobbing prevented her from saying any more. Joanes was at the foot of the bed, ready to help in any way he could. He was waiting for the professor to console his wife, but instead the old man stood there, snorting through his nose.

"Don't get all sentimental," he told his wife. "If this man is so kind and generous, why hasn't he let us use his phone to call our son?"

Her sobs stopped in a flash. Joanes looked at the professor, petrified.

"He has a telephone?" asked the woman.

"He sure does," answered her husband.

The professor's wife looked at Joanes, her eyes wide open and her jaw trembling.

"I've already told you that my phone ran out of battery," replied Joanes.

"It's not true," said the professor. "And don't insult me like that, lying to my face. Don't you dare. Your telephone is still working."

"He has a telephone?" repeated the woman.

"I just told you he does, are you deaf?" responded her husband, not looking at her, and his eyes locked on Joanes. "And now I'd like to know why he won't let us use it, what critical motive is preventing him from lending it to us."

"I'll say it again—my phone is out of battery."

"You know as well as I do that's not true."

The professor's wife heaved herself across the sheets toward Joanes.

"Please . . . I have to know how my son is."

Joanes backed off, as if afraid of her touch.

"Please, I'm begging you. I have to know if he's OK!"

The professor held his stony expression.

Joanes threw up his hands, trying to appease the situation.

"I need the phone," he said, categorically.

"You need it," said the professor.

"That's right."

"For what, may I ask?"

"I'm expecting a call."

"From your family?"

"An important call."

"Even though the system's overloaded."

"That's right," repeated Joanes, now less certain.

"Which is to say that your phone is still in working order. Perhaps because it's a satellite phone?"

Joanes didn't answer.

"What does that mean?" asked the woman, unnerved by the silence that followed. "What was that about the phone?"

"What it means," explained the professor, "is that with this kind of phone, it makes no difference if the network's overloaded. What it means is that the phone is perfectly usable."

The professor's wife immediately redoubled her pleading.

"There's hardly any battery left at all," said Joanes, remaining firm. "Just enough for one call. And I need it."

The woman seemed not to have heard him. She begged, her face bathed in tears.

"Why is this call so important?" the professor demanded to know.

His calm tone was somehow far more unsettling than his wife's supplications.

"Why haven't you made the call already?"

"It's not a call I have to make. It's one I'm waiting for," Joanes explained. "A professional matter."

"Would you care to elaborate?" asked the professor. "I believe the situation calls for an explanation."

"All you need to know is that it's an important call for my business. If it weren't the case, I'd have already lent you the phone, I assure you."

"But . . . my child!" implored the professor's wife.

"I'm sorry," said Joanes. "Maybe your husband will be able to get ahold of another phone. There are several people in the hotel that—"

"This professional call," interrupted the professor, "it's more important than a person's life?"

"Forgive me, but, from what I've heard, your son's life does not depend on you calling him. He'll live or he'll die, phone call or no."

On hearing this, the professor's wife buried her face in the pillow, and her entire body collapsed into great, sobbing heaves.

The professor was unmoved. Staring at Joanes, he said, "You cannot imagine what I can achieve with a simple phone call."

Joanes took a deep breath, looked at his hands, and dried his palms on his pants. He contemplated the tiled floor for a second and said, "In that case, I'm very pleased for you. All you have to do is get ahold of a phone, and all your problems will be solved. But it won't be mine."

He got back down on the floor, leaning his back against the wall, and sat glaring into a corner of the room.

The professor looked at him in disgust and turned his attention to his wife. He rubbed her back and whispered soothing words—quite unconvincingly—in her ear. After a while she drew her face away from the pillow and muttered something. The professor put his face right up against hers in order to make out what she was saying. Then he said, "Of course," and his wife buried her head back in the pillow.

The professor got to his feet and addressed Joanes.

"My wife would like to be alone for a moment, if you would be so kind. Given that you cannot lend us the telephone, perhaps the least you could do is grant us this small request. We'd like to have a moment alone."

Joanes grabbed his backpack and reluctantly got to his feet.

Some candles stuck in jars were the only form of lighting in the living room. The hotel owner had a prime position among the many people in the room—a massage chair right in front of the television. Neither, however, was working. He spent a while fiddling with the dial on the portable radio, hoping to find a station without interference, but he gave up and switched it off.

"Saves the battery," he said.

The living room was packed. As well as the people sitting on chairs and sofas, there were dozens of others on the floor. Joanes was among them. They'd provided seat cushions to make them more comfortable, but the room was boiling, and the cushions seemed to make it even hotter. There were two babies in a little playpen. At least one of them needed a change of diaper. A huge, sour-faced woman, who was in charge of the hotel storeroom, appeared carrying bottles of water whose seals were broken and took away the empty ones. Several of the Mexican guests were nibbling on strips of jerky. Another had a guitar in his arms; he didn't play a single note, just held it against himself tightly. Various conversations were going on at once, and Joanes only joined in when someone addressed him directly.

It was already completely dark out, and raining. Every now and then the conversations fell quiet, and then you could hear the wind. It didn't seem to Joanes to be blowing especially hard. He'd felt stronger gales. This one wasn't making him feel particularly vulnerable. It wasn't really clear why they were all there, cooped up in that hotel. He had to close his eyes and do some breathing exercises to suppress the urge to go outside, get into the car, and disappear.

Another silence, longer than the previous ones, made him open his eyes. The professor was standing by the door, looking at the scene before him with a look of revulsion on his face. He made a sign to Joanes.

"May we speak a minute?"

Joanes got up and walked out, all eyes in the room on him.

He followed the professor to the lobby. They were alone. The space was being used as a storage area for all the chairs and tables that had been out in the yard earlier. The professor took two chairs and placed them next to each other. He signaled at Joanes to take a seat.

"I think you and I ought to talk things through a bit more calmly."

Joanes sat down.

"I went too far," began the professor, also taking a seat. "I shouldn't have asked you for the phone in front of my wife. It was tactless, and I'm genuinely sorry. But I'm sure you understand that both my wife and I are under serious pressure. I apologize. We're all human, right?"

He smiled at Joanes as he said this. Then he wiped his palms along his pant legs and tried to straighten out the creases, which were considerably faded from the day's wear.

"How's your wife?" asked Joanes.

"I gave her a sedative, and she's sleeping a little."

"I've tried to get ahold of a telephone for you, but the owner of the hotel swears the network's overloaded. He has personally offered to lend you his phone later, once communications are back up. He promised me."

The professor took a deep breath and slowly let the air out.

"Thank you."

"Don't mention it."

After a pause, the professor said, "You were a student of mine."

"That's right."

"Could you remind me when?"

Joanes reminded him, and the professor wrinkled his brow trying to remember.

"I'm sorry. I don't remember you. A good number of you passed through those classrooms. I hope I didn't make things too hard for you. I know that neither I nor my course had a very good reputation among the students."

"I didn't have any trouble passing. In fact, I was crazy about Numerical Analysis," said Joanes with a sheepish smile.

"You liked it? A lot? Well . . . it's not often you hear that. Where do you work now?"

"I run my own business. Air conditioning units."

The professor frowned.

"Air conditioning."

"That's right."

"What's your business called?"

Joanes told the professor, who shook his head.

"I'm not familiar with it."

Joanes gave him a few more details, like the brands he used as his suppliers and the names of a few big clients—health care centers, banks, and supermarket chains, most of them from back when he'd shared the running of the business with his friend.

"Sounds like things are going remarkably well," said the professor. "I'm really pleased for you."

"Can't complain."

"I've never worked for myself. I imagine it must be very gratifying. Above all when business is booming."

"Without a doubt."

"Would you say you're satisfied?"

There was a pause before Joanes replied, "I'm sorry, I don't catch your drift."

"Satisfied with your professional life. With the decisions you've made."

"Of course I am. Very satisfied. I make my own decisions."

"That's important to you."

Joanes gave a firm nod and added, "A lot of people would like to be in my position."

"I don't doubt that for a moment. Especially since things are going so well."

Joanes nodded again.

The professor removed his glasses and rubbed the lenses with his shirttail. Then, as if he were merely thinking out loud, he said, "Before, in the room, I was under the impression that you were in some sort of trouble. That is, professional trouble. Something about your insistence on keeping the phone."

"I'm waiting for an important call."

"Yes, that much was made perfectly clear. But when you said that it was important, I imagined it was something crucial."

"Precisely."

"But now you're telling me you're the owner of your own business, so I suppose this 'crucial' refers to the fact that the future of the business depends, to a great extent, on this phone call."

Joanes didn't say a word.

"And yet, you've just told me that your business is thriving."

"I'm waiting for a call from an important client. But my business doesn't depend on it."

"I see. But it is sufficiently important a call for you not to lend me your phone for even a minute."

"I'm afraid so. I have my reasons for not giving it to you."

"I don't doubt your reasons. I understand that in circumstances such as these, having access to some means of communication is essential. For example, to be able to get ahold of your family. Who knows how long we'll be stuck in this place. It's perfectly understandable that you should want to keep the phone for yourself, and only for yourself. Anyone in your shoes would do the same."

"I'm afraid you're right," Joanes responded, although he didn't sound convinced.

"That's why it was wrong of me to ask you for it the way I did. In front of my wife. To submit you to that, let's say, emotional strain. Because my wife isn't able to rationalize the situation as I have just done, traumatized as she is just now. She wouldn't understand your reasons."

The professor pulled his chair in closer toward Joanes. Lowering his voice, with a complicit smile, he said, "But now, with no one around to hear us, I'm asking you again for your telephone."

To underscore his words, he pointed to the backpack, which Joanes hadn't once let out of his sight.

"We'll keep the whole thing between me and you," he went on. "Between two practical people. I'll try to be as brief as possible. And as for what I'm able to find out, if it's good news, I'll share it with my wife. But if it's not such good news ... well, I'll keep it to myself, for now. We're not exactly in the most appropriate place for her to find out that ... well, you understand me, right?"

"I can see you've thought of everything."

"I try. I understand that if your phone runs out on you, it could be inconvenient for the reasons we've discussed, but you can get ahold of one in this hotel easily. And most likely tomorrow the weather will have improved a bit, and we'll all be able to get out of here. Try to understand, I can't just sit here and give up hope of finding out what's happened to my son. I have to try right now. I'm asking you to put yourself in my place and imagine if it were your son who—"

"I can imagine it perfectly well," interrupted Joanes. "But it's out of the question. As I've already told you—"

"You have your reasons."

"That's right."

The professor let out a sigh and rested his elbows on his knees. He stayed there for a moment or two. Joanes knew he was planning his next assault and kept quiet, preparing himself for whatever might be thrown at him.

When he straightened up again, the professor's smile was one of resignation.

"I suppose I can't influence your decision with a little incentive."

"You're talking about money? You want to pay me?"

"I know it's uncouth, but yes."

"No," Joanes replied steadfastly. "I'm not going to change my mind."

"That's what I thought. And what I imagined, too, coming from someone of your integrity, and a former student of mine, at that. That's why I'm begging you, for my son and for my wife. You know me, so you know I wouldn't normally ask in such a way."

Barely audibly, Joanes responded, "I'm so sorry, but the answer is still the same."

The professor nodded and sat back in his chair.

"I understand," he said, "and I hope you understand that I had to try."

"Of course I understand. I'm very sorry for the situation you're both in."

The two men were silent for a moment. The conversations in the nearby bedrooms and living room were muffled by the wind, which was whipping against the hotel door, making it clatter against its frame. Joanes felt calmer now that they'd cleared things up. He was pleased with the way he'd handled the situation and thought that, despite the painfulness of the situation, the professor, too, felt better. Joanes hadn't let his emotions get the better of him. He'd remained true to the pragmatism that the professor so valued and had tried hard to inculcate in his students. Joanes had given him reason to be proud of him.

"I have to be honest with you," said the professor, interrupting Joanes's train of thought. "The truth is that I do remember you. I remember perfectly well."

There was a pause, then he went on.

"I remember that you came to see me at my home. It was a Saturday, in the morning. The weather was bad, but we sat out on the balcony. You were about to start working for Robot Systems, a business that was going strong in those days. I was very pleased that one of my students should have gotten a position like that at such a young age. I found out later that there'd been some kind of problem. It was a shame. I was pretty sorry about it. I ought to apologize for lying before about not remembering you. But I thought that by admitting to remembering you and our meeting and what happened afterward, I would bring back bad memories for you. But now you tell me things are going excellently, so I have no reason to worry."

Joanes listened in disbelief. The professor went on speaking.

"I've been retired for several years, but a few companies still request my services as a consultant. By which I mean that I've held on to my contacts. And I was thinking that, even though your business is doing splendidly, a bit of extra help never does any harm. I could talk to some of those contacts. Several of them owe me serious favors. I could put in a good word for your business, make a few calls. Of course, not right now, but later on, once the dust has settled. What do you say?"

Joanes couldn't reply. He was too busy processing what he'd just heard, trying to reconcile what the professor had just told him with his own memories and the fantasies he'd developed over the years. The professor took his silence as an invitation to go on speaking.

"You might also be interested in trying your hand at something new. Before, in the room, I noticed you were particularly interested in what we were discussing. You've clearly kept your finger on the pulse and not limited yourself to your own specific area of business. You presented some ideas back there that, even if I don't exactly agree with them, were undoubtedly interesting. You tick all the right boxes for succeeding at a new challenge. Something more meaningful than an air conditioning business, and, please don't take offence, better looked upon by your colleagues. Something akin to the role you would have had at Robot Systems, if things hadn't worked out the way they did."

The professor spoke slowly, lending weight to his words and ensuring that Joanes was absolutely clear about what he was offering. Joanes stayed glued to his seat, his hands resting limply on his thighs.

"I can offer you that, too. The chance to start again, if you wish. In return, you already know what I'm asking—something very simple, so simple we can resolve it right here, in an instant."

A loud clatter, like something collapsing, startled the congregation in the living room. A few of them leapt to their feet to see what had happened. The rest, delighted that something had finally livened up the tedious evening, followed them.

The chairs that had been stacked in piles were now strewn across the lobby floor, and in among them sat the professor, checking to see if his glasses were broken. His lip was bleeding. Joanes was watching him with his arms hanging limply at his sides. The Mexican guests formed a circle around them both. The hotel owner, slowed by his limp, cleared a way through the crowd to get to Joanes. He assessed the scene and then turned to the professor, who was struggling to get to his feet.

"What happened?"

Joanes, his eyes fixed on the professor, didn't answer. The professor rejected the help of two Mexican men who were trying to get him to his feet.

"I'm fine," he said. "Don't worry."

"Did you punch him?" the hotel owner asked Joanes.

It was the professor who answered.

"Nothing's happened. I simply tripped and fell against the chairs. A clumsy accident."

The hotel owner looked at him incredulously.

"Is that what happened?" he asked Joanes.

Joanes didn't answer.

Several people in the crowd had begun to whisper, and the hotel owner silenced them with an authoritative gesture.

"Don't you have anything to say, sir?"

"Leave him be," said the professor. "This is between us. We're all under a lot of pressure today."

The hotel owner didn't let that put him off.

"I have no intention of leaving him be," he said. "You, sirs, are currently in my establishment, and I don't put up with anyone fighting in front of my guests or my family."

He paused, in case either of the accused had something to add. Since they didn't, he added, "I won't allow this kind of behavior under my roof. I'm very sorry, but whoever's responsible will have to leave."

He spoke firmly, asserting all his professional authority.

"You're throwing me out?" asked Joanes, snapping out of his silence for the first time.

"Nobody fights under my roof without consequences."

The professor scoffed at the hotel owner.

"Nobody's fought anyone here. Didn't you hear what I said? I fell over."

"Let this man speak for himself," replied the hotel owner.

"Fine by me," said Joanes. "I don't want to stay here a minute longer."

"What are you talking about?" cried the professor. "You can't be serious. Where will you go?"

"There's a place," said the hotel owner. "Back on the road to Los Tigres, you go down a couple of miles. On the left you'll see a cabin. They put it up for the construction workers who were meant to build a hotel nearby. But the project didn't go ahead, and now the cabin is empty."

"A cabin?"

"It has brick walls and a solid roof," said the owner. "It'll hold out against the wind."

"But how's he going to get there?" asked the professor.

"Have you all lost your minds? We're in the middle of a hurricane!"

"It's no big deal," said Joanes. "I said I'm leaving."

The professor pleaded with him to calm down. He asked everyone present to calm down.

"Let's talk about this. You and I."

"I don't want to talk to you again."

"I know. But I'm asking you as a favor. Think about this for a moment. You don't need to do this."

Joanes didn't respond, so the professor asked the others to give them a moment alone. The hotel owner nodded and told the rest to return to their rooms. The Mexican guests left grudgingly. Some of them held back to try to catch what they could of the conversation.

Joanes gave the professor a look as if to say "get on with it."

"There's no need for you to leave. We can talk to that man, to the owner. I'm sure he'll put you up in another room if you don't want to stay with us."

"That's all you have to say?"

"Ah, so you think I owe you an apology? The right thing would be for *you* to apologize to *me*."

"Don't *you* speak to me about what's right or wrong."

"I'm not following you."

"Forget it," said Joanes, walking off. "I'm out of here."

"No. Wait. Before you go, we need to get everything out in the open."

Joanes stopped.

"Go on."

"Everything I said is true. I can help you. I don't understand why you reacted the way you did. Perhaps you thought I was talking down to you. But that's not the case. I only want to help you, in return for you helping me."

"This is what you wanted to get out in the open?"

"Well what else? I have to find out how my son is. I'll do whatever it takes. I have to know if the explosion left him badly injured, or if—"

"What explosion?" interjected Joanes. "You told me it was a diving accident."

"It was both," hastened the professor. "A diving accident and an explosion. I don't know the details. You see why I have to speak to my son, or with someone who knows something?"

Very slowly, a smile was spreading across Joanes's face.

"What is it?" asked the professor, clearly offended.

"You're lying to me."

"Excuse me?"

"None of this is true. This story about your son in Egypt, with the explosions and all the rest, it's not true."

The professor turned red.

"You're doing it again," Joanes continued. "You're lying to me. I don't know why, but you are. Who knows why you want my phone. You're a liar, a manipulator. You always have been. For as long as I've known you. A manipulator," he repeated.

"How dare you!"

Joanes shook his head, still smiling.

"I should never have given you the time of day. Not now, not then."

And with that, he walked off.

"Come back here! Don't be a fool!"

"Do *not* call me a fool!" answered Joanes, who turned, grabbed the professor by his shirtfront, and began to shake him.

The Mexican guests in the hallway started shouting, and two of them ran over to pull the men apart. The hotel owner followed as fast as his lame leg would carry him.

"Enough already! I want you out of my house, now! Both of you!"

"I'm not going anywhere," replied the professor. "My wife isn't well."

Three of the hotel owner's relatives stepped forward. One of them was well over six feet tall. He wore a sleeveless shirt, and you could see his muscly, heavily tattooed arms and shoulders plainly. He was holding a beer can in his hand, flexing his arm to show off his biceps.

"What's the problem, man? Didn't you hear my uncle?"

The hotel owner held up his arm, calling for calm.

"You have to go," he insisted.

"But, my wife . . ." began the professor, clearly worried.

"What's wrong, old man?" Joanes cut in. "You scared? It's just a little storm."

The professor's cheeks went red again.

"If you're considering staying," continued Joanes, "remember you don't have any money to pay for the room. You spent it all trying to get ahold of your son. The one who had an accident."

The hotel owner accompanied Joanes to the storeroom, where he handed him a kerosene lamp, a box of matches, three blankets that had been darned and re-darned innumerable times and gave off a thick stench of damp, three bottles of water, and something to eat.

"That'll keep you going till tomorrow morning."

Joanes felt the weight of the lamp.

"It's half empty."

The hotel owner scratched his lame leg and shrugged his shoulders.

"That's all there is."

"Right, that's all there is," said Joanes, who gave the owner a few pesos in exchange for the bundle of things.

"And the money for the room."

"Don't even think about it."

The hotel owner held his gaze but in the end let it go.

The lobby was heaving. Most of the guests had congregated there to witness their departure. The professor turned up, pushing his wife in her wheelchair. Far from seeming shocked or worried, she was smiling a kind of resigned smile. When she reached Joanes's side, she told him, "I knew it would come to this."

One of the Mexican women offered her a waterproof poncho. The professor's wife looked at her suspiciously but then took it, muttering a few words of thanks.

"You're going to need this," the hotel owner told Joanes, handing him a flashlight. "You should head out first. Bring the car around so it'll be easier for them to . . . you know."

He pointed to the wheelchair.

Joanes nodded and put his rain jacket over his head and shoulders. The hotel owner went and stood by the door. When Joanes gave him the sign, the hotel owner unbolted the door and opened it. The wind and slashing rain flew straight into the lobby, driving back the crowd. Within seconds, the floor was plastered with water, leaves, and branches.

"Go!" bellowed the hotel owner.

Joanes hesitated, taken aback by the howling of the storm. Then, clutching his backpack to his body, he dipped his head and launched himself into the darkness.

The hotel owner needed the help of one of his relatives to close the door. Then all eyes turned on the professor, who stared back at them without the slightest hint of emotion.

119

He made for the car as fast as he could. The front lawn had turned into a quagmire. The beam of the flashlight barely penetrated the darkness.

Once inside the car, he sat motionless behind the wheel, catching his breath. It was as if invisible hands were hurling buckets of water at the windshield. He said to himself that this wasn't exactly a hurricane. Just a storm. And it would weaken in strength as it traveled north.

He also told himself that it would be pretty easy to bolt right then and there, without the professor. He only had to start the engine and go. They'd look after the man and his wife at the hotel.

He started the car. As he turned on the headlights, he saw, just beyond the lawn, the thick undergrowth thrashing about like a choppy ocean.

The current wasn't as strong at the guide had led them to believe, but even so, the professor's son didn't let go of the cable during his descent. He followed the wake of bubbles left by his partner, a few yards ahead of him. Visibility was good. They soon caught sight of the boat wreck. The cable guide was fixed to one of the deck rails. More bubbles, this time emerging out of the hulk's various orifices, told them there were more divers inside.

The SS Thistlegorm sank on October 6, 1941, in the northern part of the Red Sea, while en route to Alexandria, where it was taking supplies to the allied forces in Egypt. It was spotted by a pair of German bombers who were returning to their base in Crete after completing a mission. The planes were almost out of fuel, so they wasted no time. They launched straight at the boat. The bombs went through the deck and all the way down to the hold, where they exploded, splitting the freighter in two. Nine of the forty-one crew members died in the shipwreck.

The boat was covered with a bulbous layer of rust, corals, and sponges. The professor's son saw a moray eel emerge from the open mouth of a deck canon, which was now the animal's fixed abode. On the sandy sea bed, not far from the boat, lay one of the two locomotives that the SS Thistlegorm had been transporting for Egyptian National Railways. It was tempting, but there'd be time for that later.

His partner caught his attention and pointed toward a hatch. The professor's son nodded. They switched on their flashlights and swam down into the hold.

Everything was brown inside the boat. The beams from the flashlights lit a narrow passageway. What looked like particles suspended in the water proved on closer inspection to be a shoal of tiny fish the same color as the rust on the bulkhead.

The SS Thistlegorm *had been carrying a wide array of cargo—rain boots, trucks, armored vehicles, radio equipment, rifles . . . In the hold, the floor was covered by a jumbled mess of debris that looked like trash piled up by floodwaters. The two divers moved carefully, so as not to disturb the sediment. They spotted a row of Norton motorcycles leaning one against the other, like books on a shelf. The professor's son fiddled with his underwater camera to photograph a scorpionfish posing on one of the seats. His partner signaled for them to move on. They swam around the hold for a while and then left again through one of the bomb holes in the hulk. They continued exploring the freighter and taking photos until their air gauges told them it was time to go back.*

They followed the cable guide as they made their ascent. It ended in a buoy, and just next to that was the boat. Their Egyptian guide gave them a hand hoisting themselves onto the platform at the stern.

"Everything OK?"

The professor's son gave two thumbs up. His partner took off his tank, which the guide then put in the rack set into the side of the vessel. He did the same with the professor's son's tank.

"Something to drink now?"

The two men nodded.

They took off their wetsuits, and the guide grabbed a couple of beers from the cooler. He took another for himself and sat down at the helm.

The professor's son and his partner drank as they recounted the dive. There were other diving boats anchored around the buoy.

They ate something and then took a dip in the nude, not caring that they could be seen by the other boats. The professor's son got out of the water with a cheeky laugh and went into the cabin. His partner followed him. They closed the door.

The guide didn't pay them any attention. It wasn't the first time he had a pair of fully-grown men fooling around like kids and having a kiss and a cuddle. What's more, they'd accepted his boat rental price without any haggling, and his instinct told him they'd probably leave a decent tip, too. He killed time reading the previous day's paper. Eventually his passengers came out of the cabin and told him they were ready to do another dive.

"The locomotive now?"

They nodded.

At the stern end of the deck, the professor's son squeezed into his wetsuit. His partner went back into the cabin.

"I'm gonna grab my other goggles," he said. "These ones pinch my nose."

From among the various tanks, the guide chose a full one. It had spent all morning in the sun, its contents expanding in the heat. This fact in itself wasn't enough to cause what happened next. But the tank was old, and it had a crack where the cylinder joined the air valve. When the guide put it down on the deck with a little thump, the bottle exploded.

In the cabin, the explosion threw the professor's son's partner against a bulkhead. He got up, stunned. He was bleeding from the forehead, and there was a sharp buzzing in his ears. He staggered out on deck, which was stained red with the guide's blood. There were pieces of him stuck to the gunwale and others floating in the sea, in pink patches of water. The professor's son was also in the water, having been propelled outward by the explosion. He wasn't moving, and was floating facedown.

His partner leaped into the water after him.

PART III

Cabin

Joanes drove leaning into the wheel. The wind and rain lashed against the car. They came off the small lane that led to the hotel, turned onto the Los Tigres road, and followed it away from the town, which disappeared into the distance. They made slow progress due to the almost total invisibility and the branches strewn across the road.

"Keep your eyes peeled," said Joanes. "The cabin should be on the left."

In the back seat, the professor's wife pressed her nose against the window next to her, but she couldn't see a thing. Her husband passed her the flashlight, and she shone it at the passing roadside.

"See it?"

"Not yet."

The wind sent a garden chair flying out of nowhere, and it smashed into the side of the car, making all three of them jump. A nightgown, presumably belonging to some lady from Los Tigres, went flying past the headlights, all puffed up in the wind, its sleeves flailing wildly.

"Focus!" the professor told his wife. "It must be around here somewhere."

"You don't think we already passed it back there, do you?"

Nobody answered.

A hundred or so yards further along, the woman shouted, "There! There's something over there!"

Joanes braked suddenly and looked to where the flashlight was shining. He couldn't see more than a track coming off the main road. The light didn't reach any further than that.

"Do you think that's it?" asked the professor's wife.

"We're going to have to risk it," replied Joanes.

He turned onto the side street, which was narrow, riddled with potholes, and almost completely choked with vegetation. They pressed on, crushing branches and praying they wouldn't get stuck.

"There!" they cried all together.

A one-story building, the windows boarded up. Joanes stopped the car in front of the door, which was closed but rattling inside its frame in the wind.

"Give me the flashlight," he told the woman.

He jumped out of the car and ran toward the cabin, which was raised above the ground on a platform about a foot and a half high. A couple of steps led up to the entrance. At some point a lock had protected the door, but it had been wrenched off a long time ago. Somebody had passed a piece of rope through the remaining hole and attached it to a hook on the front of the building. Joanes removed the rope, and the wind shot the door open. He gave the place a quick once over and went back to the car.

"We'll carry your wife in together," he told the professor. "The chair stays in the trunk."

They carried the woman to the cabin, splashing through the soaking mush of leaves. They left her on a metal bed base whose one missing leg had been replaced by a few bricks and on top of which lay a grayish mattress smattered with stains. It was the only piece of furniture in the cabin.

Joanes went back one last time to the car for the blankets and the rest of the things that the hotel owner had given them. The next priority was to close the cabin's door in such a way that it would stay closed. On the inside of the wall there was another hook, and Joanes wound the rope around it. The door banged fiercely against the frame, and it looked like the rope wouldn't hold out for long. On the floor there were several more boards like those covering the windows. He chose the one that seemed most resistant and used it to buttress the door. All the while, the professor shone the flashlight on Joanes. The door stopped rattling, and the noise of the wind dimmed.

Having done all this, Joanes could finally take a proper look at the place where they were going to spend the night.

It smelled of damp, of stagnant air, of rot, and of something else, which the three of them could only associate with excrement. The biggest room took up almost the entire surface area of the cabin and, given its size, they guessed it was where whomever the construction had been built for had slept, if indeed it had ever been occupied. Another room, tucked away in a corner at one end of the building, was closed off to them by a metal door. Joanes pushed the door, and it gave a little groan as it swung open. There before him was an empty, windowless space, just a few feet long on each side. He guessed that at some point it had been intended as an office or storeroom.

The bathrooms were on the other side of the cabin. There were three showers, another three more stalls for the toilets, and a couple of sinks. The stalls didn't have doors, and if at some point they'd had toilets, someone had long since done away with them. Only the plumbing pipes were left, jutting out of the wall, along with some holes in the grounds, holes which someone had used not too long ago. Of course, there was no water. In the corner lay the remains—the skin and a muddle of bones—of what might have been a possum. The whole cabin had a polished cement floor.

That was it.

Some rusty cans of food, bottles, and other trash were littered across the floor, signs that other guests sometimes stopped by the cabin. This worried Joanes, who then double-checked that the door and windows were firmly shut. Whoever had blocked the windows had done so with great care. At least they'd be protected from the rain.

The scene was so dismal that Joanes preferred to keep his mouth shut. He didn't want to overstress the place's obvious deficiencies, and he guessed from the others' silence that they felt the same. The darkness and the storm only intensified the poor impression the cabin made on them. Joanes forced himself to see it another way, with new eyes—with a little sweep of the floor and some sunshine, the place wouldn't be so bad. The walls were painted a pistachio color, and on the upper part, skirting the ceiling, some well-intentioned if poorly skilled person had begun to draw a decorative border of vines and tropical birds.

The professor held up his wife, while Joanes turned the mattress, hoping—in vain—to find fewer stains on the other side, and then spread one of the blankets over it.

"You can lie down now," he told the woman.

The professor put her down on the bed. Afterward, he lit the oil lamp and, carrying the lamp and his luggage, took himself off to the bathroom to put on a dry change of clothes.

"The hotel room was a positive suite compared to this," said the woman once she and Joanes were alone.

He kicked away the garbage around the foot of the bed. A blanket of dead cochineals—their shells parched and curled into little balls—crunched under the soles of his feet. On the floor, the flashlight lit up a V shape of dust and grime, over which a rust-colored millipede was crawling. Joanes remembered the chronicles he'd read of the conquistadors, which told of flies that bit people inside their noses and ears, bites that would later become infected and swell up terribly, and of worms that crawled onto sleeping people at night and burrowed through their eyelids and eyes.

He shook these thoughts from his head.

"It's not so bad," he replied. "I'd imagined some shed that the wind would rip apart piece by piece. This seems solid, at least."

He took off his rain jacket and patted himself dry with one of the blankets.

"We should have stayed at the hotel," said the professor's wife. "Whatever the cost."

Joanes said nothing.

"You don't think a tree could fall on us?" she asked.

"Not windy enough."

When the professor came back from the bathroom, he was carrying a metal bucket, which was swinging by its handle from one of his fingers.

"I found this. Whoever was here before used it to make a fire. We could do the same."

He had a point. The hurricane had made the temperature drop. The woman, who was wrapped up in one of the blankets, was shivering.

"Here, indoors?" she asked. "Won't the smoke asphyxiate us?"

"There are too many air currents for that," answered her husband.

Someone had pierced holes in the bucket to help the fire catch. It was black with soot, and the base was covered in a dark, gritty residue. Joanes and the professor surveyed the trash around the cabin, searching for something that would burn. They decided on the boards that were strewn across the floor. They propped them up diagonally, resting one end on the floor and the other against the wall, and then stamped on them so they snapped in the middle. They kept going until they had a decent amount of firewood.

Joanes placed the bucket near the bed and added the smallest pieces of wood to it.

"It's too damp," said the professor. "It'll need something else if it's going to catch."

There was nothing suitable in the cabin. Joanes opened his backpack and pulled out the notebook where he'd made his notes about the reduction to the hotel offer the night before. He tore off a few blank pages, scrunched them into balls, and put them inside the bucket, under the sticks of wood. He held a lighter to them. The wood resisted. Joanes was forced to go on tearing out pages until he reached those where his notes were written. He tore them out, too. At last, the wood caught fire. It let off a load of smoke, and the residue at the bottom of the bucket gave off an acrid stench as it melted. But the fire gave them light and heat. The professor turned off the flashlight.

The three of them watched the flames in silence.

In spite of the cabin, the hurricane, and the exhaustion, Joanes was pretty pleased with himself. He'd shown conviction. He was sure that nobody expected that when the hotel owner told him get out, his response would be a cool "fine by me." He felt a certain degree of pride at spending the night in that place, in the middle of the wilderness and a Category 2 or even Category 3 hurricane.

He thought about the telephone call he'd been waiting for all day. There in the cabin, in the thick of night, surrounded by the whistling wind, all of that seemed a million miles away. And then, as he watched the fire, he realized with absolute certainty that the call was never going to come, that he would never supply air conditioning to that hotel. To his surprise, it didn't bother him in the slightest. He told himself that his business would survive. And if that wasn't the case, well, that didn't matter, either, because he'd find a way to keep going.

As soon as he'd warmed himself up a bit, he moved away from the professor and his wife. With the intention of catching a few winks, he sat down on the floor with his back against one wall, stretched his legs, and closed his eyes.

He imagined himself adrift in the waters of the Caribbean, lying on a piece of driftwood, a fragment of some vessel or another. He was exhausted, on the brink of passing out. He'd spent hours at the mercy of the waves and currents. He could hardly keep his head above the surface.

Then an island appeared. It was very close, but until that moment he hadn't been able to see it. The current gently drove him toward it. He was escorted by a flock of shrill seagulls flying above him.

The waves left him on a deserted beach. His legs could barely support the weight of his body when he set foot on the sand. He stumbled a few steps forward, just enough to reach the shade of a jungle of coconut trees, where at last he could collapse to the ground and give in to his tiredness. Coconuts thumping against the sand as they fell from the trees were the heartbeats of his sleep. Red crabs scurried around with pincers raised, like frightened Lilliputians, not daring to touch him.

"Did you two hear that?" asked the professor's wife.

Her husband, who was sitting on the floor next to her, looked at her wearily. Joanes opened his eyes. They couldn't hear anything other than the wind and the rustle of the vegetation outside.

"It was probably a branch snapping," said the professor.

"It wasn't a branch. It sounded like something metallic. Like jangling."

They listened again, but couldn't hear anything like jangling.

"It could have been anything. The wind dragging along some—" began Joanes.

But he was interrupted by a noise coming from outside. Sure enough, it was a metallic jangling. It sounded close. Next thing they knew, they heard a deep, masculine voice ordering someone to keep walking and then reassuring him, saying, "We're here now."

A moment later, the door rattled. Someone had pushed it from the outside.

"What the fuck!"

More blows came and almost brought down the door.

"Manco! Beluga! Are you in there?"

Inside, nobody said a word. They watched the door, their hearts beating hard in their chests.

"Open the door, you sons of bitches! Can't you see it's us? We're going to drown out here!"

"Don't open it," the woman whispered to her husband. "If we keep quiet, they'll go away."

The professor tutted.

"They're not going to go. They'll see the fire."

The shouting stopped suddenly, and the jangling sound came back, moving around the cabin. It paused in front of a window. Whoever was outside peered through a crack in the boards.

"I can see the light! What's up with you guys? Are you going to just leave me to drown out here?"

The jangling retraced its path back to the door, and the banging started up again, this time even louder. The door shook, as if about to come off its hinges. Whoever was pushing was putting his whole weight behind him. With each bang came a whimper of pain. And still, the jangling.

Joanes got to his feet.

"What are you doing?" asked the professor.

"If he knocks it down, we're fucked."

"You're going to let him in?" asked the professor's wife.

Joanes didn't have time to answer. An even louder bang made the board bolstering the door fall to the ground. The rope still held the door closed, but there was a crack wide enough for the man to poke his head in and furiously ask, "Manco! Beluga! What the hell is up with you?"

The crack opened on the opposite side of where the group was, which meant they were in the intruder's blind spot.

Since nobody answered, the man who had been pounding on the door decided to finish the job. Through the crack, a foot-and-a-half-long machete blade poked in. The man proceeded to begin cutting the rope.

"Wait a second!" shouted Joanes, "Wait!"

He ran toward the door to rescue the rudimentary lock system that was keeping the wind and water from flooding in.

Later, he'd ask himself over and again why he'd done it, why he hadn't stopped the stranger from getting in. He could have asked the professor to help him keep the door closed. They could have shouted that there were too many people inside and that there was no room for any more. They could have buttressed the door with more boards. They could have dragged the bed over to block it. They could have done a lot of things.

He unhooked the rope. The wind swept open the door with a bang, knocking Joanes on his back. Eddies of air filled the cabin, and within a second the interior wall facing the door was splattered with leaves.

The professor was on his feet, and his wife had sat up in the bed. They watched as the soaking figure, well over six feet tall, stepped inside, looked at them one by one, and grunted, "You're not Manco and Beluga. That's for sure."

He was protected by a waterproof poncho that had been mended with strips of tape. His feet were wrapped in trash bags attached with elastic bands, and he had protected his legs with more bags, also strapped on with bands. The man was covered, shoddily but from head to toe, in plastic. He was wearing a backpack, also wrapped in trash bags, with makeshift padding on the straps made out of rubber foam. From the backpack hung a frying pan, a pot, and other odds and ends. And yet this wasn't the source of the jangling sound that followed him. In one hand he was holding the machete, and in the other a wooden cane. He placed the machete inside a leather sheath he wore on his waist and threw back the hood of his poncho.

He was a black man, his face covered with deep lines and his hair and beard woolly and gray. A chain poked out from beneath his poncho—this was the source of the jangling. It was attached to his waist. The other end of the chain was attached to the collar of a chimpanzee, which came trotting into the cabin. The monkey moved as far away from the door as the chain would allow, looking for a dry patch of ground. Once he'd found one, he crouched down and, imitating his master, looked at Joanes, the professor, and the professor's wife.

"Good evening," said the black man.

An ambiguous accent from the American South obscured his words.

Before Joanes or either of the others could react, he closed the door, pressed it shut with his shoulder, and secured it with the rope. He guessed the function of the board now lying on the floor and placed it back against the door. Then he looked around, his beard dripping wet.

"Is the lady all right?"

"She's fine," answered her husband.

"Yes, she's fine. But she can't walk," added Joanes.

The stranger chewed over this information, then simply nodded as if he understood everything now, and carried on as if he'd forgotten they were there. He left his cane leaning against the wall and, taking his time, proceeded to take off his backpack and the poncho. He removed the sheath of plastic bags from the backpack. He also took off the bags wrapped around his legs and feet. Dragging the monkey's chain behind him, he took the poncho and bags into the bathroom. When he came

137

back, he grabbed his backpack and the cane and, with the chimpanzee trotting along behind him, walked around the cabin looking for a corner that was more or less clean and dry.

Joanes had moved back to the fire with the others, and from there he didn't miss a single detail of what the new arrival and his pet were up to.

Under the poncho and the plastic bags, the stranger was wearing a pair of jeans, a T-shirt, and a jacket, which was also denim. The clothes were so filthy that they'd taken on a kind of drab, brownish hue. On his feet he was wearing a pair of heavy work boots. His pants were held up at the waist by a piece of cord, and attached to that was the machete's sheath, which he also took off before sinking to the floor with a sigh. He rested his back against the wall and closed his eyes. The monkey hopped in front of him in one swift motion. The chain swept the trash on the floor to one side. The chimpanzee sat down, attentive to his master's every move. Every now and then, he scratched his nose or looked over his shoulder at the others. He was soaked, and the water dripping from his chin formed a puddle beneath him.

"I haven't forgotten about you, my friend," said the stranger, opening his eyes.

He produced a threadbare towel from the backpack and began to carefully dry the monkey, who settled himself down between his mater's legs and closed his eyes.

"Lift your arm," said the man. "Lift it up," he repeated before raising his own left arm by way of example.

The chimpanzee copied him so that his master could dry him properly. Afterward, they repeated the routine with the other arm. As he rubbed him down with the towel, the owner said, "That's a boy. Today the heavens opened up right on top of us. Right, my friend?"

Once he'd finished with the monkey, he used the same towel to dry his own face and then wiped it across his beard and neck. He folded it, and put it away again. The man rummaged again in his backpack, this time pulling out a plastic bag, from which he then produced an onion. Using the machete, he peeled it and cut it in two, giving the group huddled around the fire ample opportunity to see the weapon in all its glory. In the places without nicks, the blade of the knife was perfectly sharpened. The handle was made of wood and had been reinforced with rope.

On seeing the master take out the onion, the chimpanzee began jumping up and down on the spot, making a few imploring squeals.

"You know it's for you. Of course it is. Come here."

The chimpanzee did as he was told, squatting back down between his master's legs, his back resting against the man's chest. The stranger set one half of the onion aside and with the other proceeded to massage the monkey, rubbing him with the side that had been cut. Not long after, the man began singing in English, in a deep, gentle voice.

"What are you doing that for?" the professor's wife wanted to know.

"Don't bother him," said her husband.

But she repeated the question. The man had stopped singing.

"The lady isn't bothering me," he said, without interrupting the massage. "I do it because it relaxes him. And after what he's been through today, he needs to relax. My very good friend here can't handle these sorts of upheavals anymore. Right, my friend?"

The chimpanzee was indeed very relaxed. He'd slowly curled into himself, and now his chin was resting on his chest. He looked like he was just about to fall asleep. His hands were resting on his knees with his palms facing up, allowing the others to appreciate how extraordinarily long his fingers were.

"I thought you were Manco and Beluga, two friends of ours who come here sometimes."

"What's the monkey called?" asked the professor's wife.

"Gagarin. Like the astronaut."

"Gagarin." She repeated.

"That's right. It's the name they gave him in the circus. At first he didn't much like it. Me neither. But we've both gotten used to it. Isn't that right, Gagarin?"

The chimpanzee threw him a sleepy glance then closed his eyes again.

"You worked in a circus? What did you do?" she wanted to know.

"That was a long time ago, ma'am," said the man. "Gagarin did what monkeys do. I cleaned and did a little of everything."

"Did you act? Can you do anything?"

"Darling," said the professor. "Don't bother the man."

The stranger laughed, a sort of broken snort through his nose. The kind of laugh you could easily mistake for an irritated sigh. He stopped stroking the chimpanzee and offered him the half onion.

"Here, buddy."

Gagarin opened his eyes, grabbed the onion slowly, and took a bite. He had enormous, yellow fangs. They could hear him chewing.

"No, ma'am, I didn't act. I wouldn't have known where to start."

"Did you look after Gagarin?"

"That I did do, yes. And I liked looking after him a lot. We became real good friends."

"Did you rub him down with onions?"

The man laughed again.

"Hear that, Gagarin? This good lady is asking if I used to rub you down. No. I learned that later on."

"Did you escape together from the circus?"

The answer took so long in coming that they all thought he wasn't going to give one. The man petted the chimpanzee, who was polishing off his half onion.

"Those sons of bitches told us they weren't earning enough money and that they were going to sell to the animals. So we left."

"Gagarin looks very tired."

"He is, ma'am. Gagarin's no spring chicken, and we've walked a long way today."

Just like his owner's, the monkey's face was covered with wrinkles. The lines of his face sunk downward, as if it were collapsing, sliding off in sheer exhaustion. His eyes were watering.

"And he seems very sad," the professor's wife added.

The stranger nodded slowly.

"You're right about that. We're both real sad. Isn't that right, my friend?"

"Why are you sad?" Joanes interjected.

"Gagarin's lost his girl. She escaped three days ago. The two of us have been looking for her ever since."

Joanes reacted without surprise. He'd already noticed some moments earlier that Gagarin's collar was exactly the same as the one worn by the chimpanzee he hit.

"How did she escape?"

"Lolita was very smart. And a bit naughty, too. She worked out how to get her chain off."

The man stopped short and gave his pet a few pats on the back.

"I'm sorry, Gagarin. I mean she *is* very smart."

The monkey gazed into the distance with what they all understood to be a pining look.

"Are we to understand that this Lolita is also a chimpanzee?" asked the professor.

"That's correct," answered the stranger.

And then he asked, "Do you mind if I make use of the fire, friends?"

"No. I guess not," replied Joanes.

From the odds and ends hanging from his backpack, the man picked out a grease-incrusted metal grill with four little support legs. He also took a pan, which he filled with water from the plastic jerry can that he was using as a canteen. Next he delved around in the backpack and took out a packet of instant soup. Carrying all of this, he moved over by the fire. He fueled it with more wood, placed the grill over the flames and the pot on top of the grill, and then sat down to wait for the water to boil. The chimpanzee stayed where he was, still linked to his master by the chain and dozy after the massage and his frugal dinner.

Joanes studied the stranger. He was an old man, or almost old. He could have been any age between fifty and seventy; his disheveled appearance made it hard to tell. Not only was his face covered in wrinkles, it also had fresh cuts and scars and infected mosquito bites on it. Two wide, gray bags hung from under his eyes. He watched the flame intensely. He looked as though he could've happily sat there in silence for the rest of the night.

"What do you three do?" the professor's wife asked him. "What do you do with your monkey friends?"

"I don't understand, ma'am."

"What she means," Joanes clarified, "is what do you do for a living."

"We do the odd show for the tourists. Things we picked up in the circus. We earn a little cash that way."

Joanes looked at the chimpanzee, who was dozing on

the floor with his legs curled up. Just like the monkey he'd hit, this one had lost some hair on several parts of his body, and in other parts the hair was gray. He was a sorry sight. Old and weary. You could see his ribs. Joanes couldn't picture him dressed up in a tutu or a clown's hat, scampering up streetlamps and capering about for the entertainment of tourists, who could have their picture taken with him for a few more pesos afterward, as a keepsake.

He could, however, imagine him wandering around Yucatán alongside his lady companion and his keeper. The two monkeys, each linked to their master by a chain. Walking ahead of the man, pulling him along if he was tired, looking out for any small morsel of food. And if they found something, no matter how hungry they were, the monkeys had to give it to their master, who would decide between eating it himself or leaving it to them. And they'd be wise to offer it to him first, because it didn't take much of an imagination to guess that the man's cane wasn't just a prop but also served as an agonizing weapon to keep them in check.

He imagined, too, the chimpanzees being forced to steal on behalf of their master, sneaking into houses through windows and making off with whatever they could. And he imagined them searching for larvae and worms under fallen tree trunks and rocks at night while their master slept, and poking sticks into anthills and putting whatever they caught in their mouths. And he also imagined them hugging one another for warmth and comfort, doing their best not to make a sound with the chains so their master wouldn't wake up and start beating them.

"Where are you from?" asked the professor. "Mississippi? Louisiana?"

The man gave him a long, blank look.

"Tuscaloosa, Alabama," he answered, his accent suddenly twice as strong.

"And how long have you lived in Mexico?"

"A lifetime, my friend."

Letting a few seconds pass to show that he appreciated the weight of this answer, the professor continued his interrogation.

"And you and your . . . colleagues usually work in this area?"

"On the coast. Where the tourists are."

"In winter, too?"

"There are always tourists here."

"I understand. Fewer during the hurricanes, isn't that so?" said the professor, pointing to the boarded up windows, behind which the wind continued to rage. "Then the tourists leave. We leave. You might have already guessed."

"Guessed what?"

"That we're tourists."

"Yes. I'd guessed as much."

"Don't you want to know why we're here?"

"None of my business."

The water in the pot had begun to boil, and the man poured in the instant soup. He pulled out a spoon from one of his pockets, rubbed it with the edge of his shirt, and stirred the mixture to dissolve the lumps. Then he took the pot with his bare hand without showing the slightest sign of pain, despite the fact that it must have been piping hot. He blew on the meager soup and took a sip. His wrinkles seemed to smoothen a little.

"I suppose you're also here because of the hurricane," said the professor.

The man eyed him over the pot, which he was slurping into noisily.

"This is nothing but a little drizzle. Now Wilma, Wilma was a hurricane. Dean, too. This is . . ."

He made a gesture with his hand, as if something unimportant were floating away into the air.

"I understand," said the professor. "But this little drizzle has put a stop to your search for your colleague."

The man assented as he stirred what remained of the soup with his spoon.

"Where did it happen? Where did you lose her?"

"In Tulum."

"Really, well, there's a coincidence! We've come from around there, too. Our hotels," said the professor, "were in Cancún."

He paused to let the information sink in. Then he added, "How long have you and the chimpanzees been together?"

"What's it to you?"

The professor shrugged his shoulders.

"It's the first time I've ever met anyone like you."

"A black man?"

The expression on the professor's face didn't move an inch.

"An ex–circus employee who's traveling Mexico in the company of two chimpanzees."

The man finished off his soup. He placed the pot to one side, wiped the spoon again with his shirt, and put it back in his pocket.

"A long time. Years."

"You must be very upset at the loss of your female companion."

The man wet his index finger and thumb with saliva and used them to remove the grill with a single, slick movement.

"Of course we're upset. Tomorrow we're going back to the coast to look for her."

"Tomorrow? This little drizzle will have stopped by then?"

"Tomorrow, the day after tomorrow . . . whenever we can, we'll go back. And now, if you'll excuse me, I'm a little tired."

The others gave a consenting nod as the man got up. He picked up the pan and pushed the grill with his foot, leaving it next to his backpack. They all watched as he unrolled a rubber matt and laid out a patched up sleeping bag on top of it. Fully clothed, without taking off his boots or untying the chimpanzee's chain, he laid down on top of the sleeping bag. Before going to sleep, he double-checked that all his belongings were within reach, especially his cane and the machete. His shuffling stirred the monkey.

"Good night, Gagarin. Sleep well."

The professor leaned in toward Joanes.

"Let's talk," he whispered. "In the other room."

"Just say whatever you have to say."

"It's better if we do it in private."

"Just tell me what it is you want to say," repeated Joanes.

The professor looked at the stranger and the chimpanzee. He gestured toward them with his eyes.

"Here? Are you sure?"

A second later, Joanes picked up the flashlight.

"Don't be long," said the wife.

Joanes walked to the adjacent room, tailed by the professor. He opened the metal door, taking care that it creak as little as possible. Once they were both inside, he closed it again. They remained standing, one in front of the other, in the middle of the little room. Joanes held the flashlight down at his side; it cast shadows over both of their faces.

"Well then?"

"I understand that our situation hasn't exactly improved over the last couple of hours. You need your telephone more than ever now, in case you need help getting out of this place."

"I thought I'd made myself clear."

"Perfectly clear. But I still need to know what's happened to my son, urgently," said the professor, who underscored his words with wild, hacking gesticulations. "You must understand. If there's something about me that displeases you, if I've offended you in some way, or if you simply don't like me, at least think of my wife. Try to imagine what she must be going through."

Joanes didn't say a word but simply looked at him in disdain, and so the professor took a deep breath and went on.

"It's better if we resolve this by talking. Just the two of us. You and I. Much better."

"It's already resolved. There's nothing more to say."

"No," said the professor firmly. "It is not resolved. Not by far. How could you possibly think it's been resolved? I want that telephone. I need it, now," he said, holding out his hand for Joanes to turn it over.

Joanes let out a laugh.

"I need it," the professor insisted. "Something serious has happened to my son. I've got a terrible feeling about it."

"A feeling? repeated Joanes. "A feeling? That's not like you. You, who are so pragmatic," he said, tapping his temple with his index finger. "Pragmatism, that's what you always drilled into us in class, remember? Of course you remember. 'Pragmatism,'" said Joanes, putting on the professor's voice. "Just like Alan Turing and his pragmatic mathematics. A good book. Very interesting. If a little biased in its contents, don't you think? But nonetheless very revealing, there's no doubt about it. Revealing in many ways. Not just of poor Turing. You know what I'm talking about."

The professor listened with a stony face. When he answered, he did so as if Joanes's words had gone in one ear and out the other, or as if he hadn't heard them at all.

"How do you think that man out there would react if he knew that you killed the monkey he's looking for?"

"Don't involve him in this. This is between us."

"Between me and you?" said the professor, raising his voice. "Of course it isn't! They are other people implicated here. For starters, the people sitting right there in the next room."

"You wouldn't dare," repeated Joanes.

"Give me the telephone. That black man out there could be dangerous. Didn't you see his machete?"

"Forget it."

The professor left the room, and Joanes stepped out after him.

"Ah, my friend!" said the professor, approaching the man. "Are you awake?"

The first one to react was the chimpanzee, who got straight to his feet and stood with his arms hanging by his sides and his legs bowed, like a gunslinger from the Wild West ready for a duel. The man opened his eyes and as a reflex snatched the machete.

"Don't touch me," he said.

The professor stopped dead in his tracks.

"Calm down, I wouldn't dream of touching you. I just want to tell you something that might be of interest."

With his free hand, the man grabbed the chain that connected him to the monkey and pulled it taut to keep Gagarin under control. Without letting go, he sat up, leaning his back against the wall.

"What do you want to tell me?"

"You see that man?" asked the professor, pointing to his former student. "You see him?"

The man nodded. From her bed, the woman asked, "What's going on? What's going on?"

"That man," the professor went on, "was out driving the day before yesterday along the costal highway, the one that skirts Tulum. That's where you lost your animal, the female. Is that correct? Good, well that man was right around Tulum when a monkey, a chimpanzee, jumped out onto the road. And he hit it with his car. He didn't kill it in the act, but he left it badly hurt. And do you know what he did next? Or, to put it correctly, what he didn't do? He didn't ask anyone for help. No one! He stayed there watching as the poor animal breathed its last breath. And then he got in his car and carried on driving as if nothing had happened."

As the professor spoke, the man got to his feet, still holding on to the monkey and the machete.

"Now, that's not exactly what happened," said Joanes, his voice tense. "I didn't stay there watching while—"

The professor interrupted him with a victorious guffaw.

"You see? He himself admits it. He hit your monkey."

"It was an accident. It wasn't my fault."

"But you admit it!"

"I hit a monkey. We don't know if it was this man's monkey."

"How many lost chimpanzees could there possible have been that day in the area?" asked the professor.

The stranger looked back and forth between the professor and Joanes. He pulled the chain tauter still, and Gagarin took a step backward. Having sensed the tension in the air, the monkey let out a screech and started to flex his legs over and over again and bare his teeth.

"It was your monkey. What did you call it before? Lolita? He killed Lolita. There's no doubt it was her. She was wearing a bracelet on her wrist. A plastic, beaded one. Did Lolita wear a bracelet like that?"

The others anxiously awaited the answer.

"Yes," said the man. "A pink and blue bracelet. She liked it a lot."

Then he said, almost talking to himself now, "I gave it to her."

"That's the one!" exclaimed the professor.

"Hang on a minute," said Joanes. "Let me explain. The monkey threw herself out onto the road. It all happened so quickly. I didn't have time to—"

"Quiet!" bellowed the man, and they all fell silent.

Then, pointing at the professor with the machete, he asked, "Why are you telling me this?"

The professor straightened up in a gesture of hurt pride.

"Because it seemed you ought to know. Ever since he killed your monkey, he's been going around telling everybody, boasting about it, bragging. As if it were something to be—"

Without even letting the professor finish his sentence, the man pointed at Joanes with the machete and said something that nobody understood—a single word, or something like a word, a series of clicks from his tongue. He let go of the chain, and Gagarin launched himself at Joanes.

Joanes barely had time to throw his arms up to protect his face. The chimpanzee pounded him with his arms and legs, all at once. Within a second, man and beast had transformed into a mass of limbs that collapsed onto the floor with a groan and the whistle of air being squeezed out of a pair of lungs. Gagarin climbed on top of Joanes's stomach. Punches like hammer blows rained down on Joanes's face.

The professor's wife began to shriek. She begged them to break it up. She begged everyone. Her husband had to hold her to stop her from falling off the bed. She looked like she was about to get up and drag herself into some corner or another for refuge. While he struggled to restrain her, the professor, equally horrified by the monkey's outburst, watched the struggle between his former student and the beast.

The monkey plunged his fist into Joanes's nose, and they all heard a crack like a branch snapping in two. Joanes retaliated, swinging a huge punch. More out of luck than anything else, the blow struck the monkey right in the stomach. The animal doubled up in pain, but the respite barely lasted a second. The chimpanzee then began jumping up and down on Joanes's testicles.

The stranger was also watching the fight, his eyes bulging, astounded by the animal's wrath. He hadn't expected him to react like this. The hand holding the chain was trembling. It was as if the chimpanzee was letting out years of accumulated anger.

"Stop it!" cried the professor. "Make it stop! Can't you see it's going to kill him?"

The man, who seemed paralyzed, didn't respond.

"Stop it!" repeated the professor. "That's enough! Are you mad?"

Between kicks and punches, Joanes managed to get the monkey off him. The animal took a starting run and jumped right back on him. This time he didn't hit him but rather sank his fangs into Joanes's left hand and shook his head as if trying to wrench it off.

"Please, please!" begged the woman. "Make it stop! We'll give you whatever you want! But get it off him!"

"Control this damn beast!" added the professor.

"Stop, Gagarin!"

But the monkey was out of his mind and didn't obey the order.

152

"Stop, Gagarin!" repeated the man, his voice quaking.

The chimpanzee didn't pay him any attention, so the man was forced to tuck the machete into the rope he used as a belt and pull the chain with both hands to separate him from Joanes.

Gagarin resisted but finally began to back off, still clutching Joanes's hand with his teeth. Joanes screamed. His hand and the monkey's mouth were attached by something resembling strings of chewing gum. Afterward, the monkey separated himself fully from Joanes, two fingers remaining clenched between his jaws.

"Come here, come here!" said the man, clearly shocked, as he pulled to gather up the chain.

Backing away, the chimpanzee dropped one of the fingers, the pinky. The man reproached him, threatening him with his fist, and the monkey glanced at him and sat down at his feet, gnawing the other finger, the ring finger, as if it were a candy bar. He was soon as calm as he'd been when he entered the cabin, as if all his rage, having claimed its due, had simply disappeared. Or as if the whole thing had been nothing more than a brief show, just to let them know what he was capable of. Now he showed an almost vainglorious indifference toward them, even his master.

On the floor, Joanes was holding his hand to his chest. Both his hand and his nose, which was broken and bent at a strange angle, were bleeding profusely. His eyes were rolling back into his head as if he were going to faint.

"Oh God, oh God, oh God," the woman repeated.

The man continued to scold the monkey. With his back bent, supplicant, he approached Joanes to ask his forgiveness and explain that he didn't mean for this to happen, that he'd only wanted to scare him a little, just a little, that he was so sorry, that he didn't know why Gagarin had reacted that way. He was so shocked, he looked on the verge of tears. Then he begged the woman's forgiveness and said that Gagarin wasn't like that, that he didn't hurt people.

He didn't get the chance to finish what he was saying. The professor, who in the meantime had picked up the cane, went up to him and thwacked him on the head.

"Shut up, old man!"

The man fell to his knees. Without knowing what had happened, he made to protect his head with his hand. He looked at the chimpanzee, but Gagarin was in his own world, impassive. The professor hit him again and the man collapsed, motionless.

Both Joanes and the professor's wife watched the scene, paralyzed.

"What did you do that for?" she asked her husband. "He was apologizing."

"I don't trust him."

Still holding on to Joanes's finger, the chimpanzee contemplated his now unconscious master. Without letting go of the cane, the professor turned toward the animal, who simply scratched his armpit, moved as far away as the chain would permit, and went on chewing the finger.

The professor crouched down next to the man to take the machete off him. Next he opened his backpack and, with a look of disgust on his face, rummaged through its contents until he found a shirt. He tore it in two and used one of the strips to tie the man's hands behind his back. With the other he gagged him, but not before tying a double knot in it, so that it would stay snug between the man's teeth.

"This way he won't be able to give the monkey any more of those orders," he explained.

He acted confidently and efficiently, as if cuffing and gagging were among his normal daily activities.

Afterward he went over to the bed and let himself flop onto it. His wife edged back to give him some space.

"Are you OK?" she asked.

He nodded, wiping the sweat from his forehead. He let go of the cane and stared, stunned, at the machete, as if he didn't know what it was. He put it down on the bed, then rubbed his hands over and again on his pant legs.

"Are you sure you're OK, darling?" the woman insisted.

Instead of responding, the professor turned to Joanes and asked, "Is there a first aid kit in that backpack of yours?"

Joanes nodded. Dragging his feet, the professor went to get the backpack. He turned on the flashlight for more light. He took out the first aid kit and examined its contents. Next he dragged Joanes over to a wall and propped him up against it.

"The hand first," he said.

He cleaned it with water, disinfected it, and then, for want of a better option, cauterized the base of the two severed fingers using silver nitrate sticks. He worked with the same care he would have shown his own son. Joanes let him. The professor bandaged Joanes's hand and mocked up a sling. Lastly, he took care of the blows to Joanes's face.

"We'll need to straighten up that nose."

But when he went to do so, Joanes recoiled, saying, "No, no . . ."

"We should do it now rather than later."

"I don't want to."

"Suit yourself. It's your nose."

Joanes's treatment left the first aid kit nearly empty. Once he'd finished, the professor got to his feet with a groan. The man was still unconscious, and his monkey didn't pay any of them the slightest attention. Joanes contemplated his pinky. To see it lying on the floor among the trash made him feel a kind of self-pity he'd never felt before. The only sound to be heard was the howling wind.

The professor put the first aid kit back in the backpack and then pulled out the satellite phone.

"Leave that alone!" said Joanes.

He tried to get to his feet, but the pain stopped him.

"It won't take more than a minute," said the professor. "It's best if you stay still."

With trembling fingers, he dialed a number and waited.

"The lines are up. It's ringing," he told his wife.

She had sat up and waited with one hand resting on her chest. She looked as though all the blood had drained from her face.

The dial tones rang for what seemed like an age. Then the professor had a kind of paroxysm when at last someone answered. He pressed the phone against his ear and covered the other one to isolate himself against the noise of the storm. Clearly anxious, he repeated a name various times, that of their son's partner.

"Is that you? I can't hear you too well . . . yes? Is that you?"

The professor told the person down the line who he was and without further ado asked about his son. He repeated the question, spacing out the words to be clear. Then he went silent.

"So, he's OK?" he asked apprehensively.

Another silence.

"What you mean is he's going to be OK."

Another pause. Then, looking at his wife with a great smile, he said, "He's out of danger."

Very slowly, she laid back down and closed her eyes.

The professor went on talking for a while, garnering more details about what had happened—the explosion of an air tank during a diving trip; the guide had died; several nearby boats had seen it all happen and someone had requested help over the radio; a helicopter didn't take long to arrive and rescue the professor's son and his partner. The professor repeated every new piece of information for the benefit of his wife.

"Yes, of course we're going to come," he said. "But we can't say when. We're still in Mexico, stuck in this hurricane. Yes . . . good . . . good . . . I'm so grateful. Please, don't let him out of your sight . . . no. For the time being there's no number you can reach me at, but I'll contact you as soon as possible . . . yes? Hello? Can you hear me? Are you still there?"

He looked at the telephone screen. The connection had gone.

"Battery's dead," he said.

He went back to his wife's side. On the way, he dropped the telephone into Joanes's backpack. The old couple hugged.

"Thank God, thank God," they said.

A few moments later, the professor pulled slowly away from her. Shaking and trying not to look either his wife or Joanes in the eye, he walked off to the adjacent room, closing the door behind him.

The professor's wife rifled around in her travel bag and pulled out a pocket mirror, which she proceeded to use to check her appearance. She sighed, then took a hairbrush and calmly ran it through her hair without taking her eyes of herself in the mirror. She behaved as if she were in her own bed, in her own room, and as if she'd forgotten everything that had gone on that night. The color had returned to her cheeks. She looked as though she were about to get up and start walking around the cabin.

"I could do with a cigarette," she said. "You don't have one, do you?"

Joanes shook his head.

"That's a shame."

"What's your husband doing in there?"

"He's crying."

Joanes glanced over toward the door to the other room in surprise. You couldn't hear a peep coming from inside.

"I'm sorry about what's happened to you," she said, "but it was necessary. You would have done the same, or worse, if you'd been in our place. You're angry right now, which is perfectly understandable, but with time you'll forget all about this. You should try to put it to the back of your mind. The storm will soon pass, and that horrible black man and his monkey will be gone. Then we'll get our story straight, a story where we all come out well. We'll say the black man tried to rob us and that you defended us. Then you'll be reunited with your family, and we'll go and look for our son. Life will go back to normal, for all of us."

"I'm not angry. I'm furious."

She gave an understanding nod.

"You'll get over it. Don't try to challenge my husband. He knows how to handle things, as you've seen for yourself. That anger you feel isn't enough. It hasn't changed you. You're still the same man you were before."

Joanes tried to get to his feet, but the pain forced him back down again. He took a deep breath, gathering his strength for a second attempt. This time he did manage to get up. He stumbled one or two steps forward and, before doing anything else, bent down to recover his pinky from the floor. He looked at it for a second and put it in his backpack. Then he moved to the bed, took the machete from where the professor had left it, and placed it in his belt. He walked over to the stranger.

"What are you doing?" she asked.

"Seeing if he's all right."

The man was still unconscious. Joanes took one of the bottles of water and poured a little on the man's face. He waited, then poured some more on his face and neck. The man groaned, opened his eyes, and then closed them again.

"How are you doing?" asked Joanes.

The man tried to move but discovered that he was tied. Gagged, he could do nothing but groan. Joanes thought then that he seemed even older than he had before.

"Can you hear me?"

The man nodded.

"When you're with your monkey and you don't want him to come near you, how do you do it?"

The man opened his eyes wide and turned his head, looking for Gagarin. He seemed to calm down when he saw him safe and well. The chimpanzee, still holding on to the remains of Joanes's ring finger, was picking things out of his fur with the tips of his own fingers, inspecting them, and then popping some of them into his mouth.

"How do you keep him at bay?" Joanes repeated.

"Why are you asking him that?" asked the woman.

"Did you not see what that animal just did to me? I want to know how to keep it under control."

And turning to face the man, he added, "Don't worry. I have no intention of hurting him."

The man gestured at the cane with his chin.

"The cane? That's what you use?"

Another nod.

Joanes took the cane and examined it. It was thick and hefty, and decorated with geometric carvings that made it look like a ritual weapon, an instrument used in sacrifices. There was a shackle fixed at the upper end and a spike at the other.

"Good," he muttered, and he proceeded to untie the chain from the man's waist.

Next, he picked out a kiwi from their small food store. Kiwi and cane in hand, he moved slowly toward the chimpanzee.

"Hello, Gagarin."

The monkey flashed him a fleeting look, more interested in his preening.

"Do you want this?"

The monkey looked at the fruit but didn't move.

"Come on. I'm sure you're still hungry."

Joanes split the kiwi open, sinking his fingers into it,

and showed the monkey the two juicy, dripping halves. The monkey gingerly stretched out his arm and took the fruit. He let the remains of the finger fall to the floor and starting munching.

Joanes gripped the cane with his healthy hand, supporting himself with the remaining fingers on his other hand, and used it to strike the chimpanzee with all his might. It hit the animal on the back of the head. The cane vibrated as if it had smashed against the concrete floor. The chimpanzee dropped the fruit and collapsed, stunned but still conscious.

The professor's wife muzzled her mouth with her fists. On the floor, the monkey's master screamed through his gag.

Joanes raised the cane into the air once more, this time striking the animal on the back. The third blow hit him again on the head. The animal stopped moving.

The creak of the door to the other room opening interrupted the stunned silence. Nothing about the professor gave away what he'd been doing in there.

"What's going on?"

"Settling some unfinished business," replied Joanes.

He pulled the chain through the shackle at the end of the cane until the tip of the stick was right against the animal's throat. Then, holding the chain taut, he hooked one of the links onto the spike at the other end. This way, if he kept a tight rein on the cane, the monkey couldn't get anywhere near him. Next he picked up his ring finger—of which only a few picked bones remained—and put it away alongside his pinky.

"Dump out my backpack," he ordered the professor.

"Why?"

"Just do what I tell you."

"I'd like to know—"

"I just want to be done with this, once and for all. I know what I'm doing. Please, do what I say."

The professor tipped the contents of the backpack onto the floor.

"Now put it over the monkey's head."

Without taking his eyes off the chimpanzee's teeth for a single second, the professor covered its head with the backpack and closed the zipper as far as he could. The result was a kind of crude hood.

"And now find something in among our friend's things to tie the monkey's hands."

The professor used a pair of black pants. He finished just as the chimpanzee began to rouse. Joanes held the cane tightly.

"You see? Your pet is just fine," he said to the man, who was sobbing with his face against the floor. Bits of trash had gotten stuck in his hair.

"I'm sorry it's come to this. But I didn't have any choice," said Joanes.

Then he added, "Do you want your monkey back?"

The man looked at him with tear-filled eyes. A thread of snot hung from his nose.

"You love him a lot, don't you? You have no one else."

The man nodded.

"You love him as if he were your son."

Another nod.

"And you loved Lolita in the same way, like a daughter. That's why losing her hit you so hard. I imagine you don't want to lose Gagarin as well. That would be too much. You'd wind up alone, with nobody to care for."

Now the man was shaking his head.

"And I'm going to give you back your monkey, and the two of you can get out of here. I know it's late at night and it's raining, but I don't think you mind, right? Just a little drizzle, as you say. Do you want to get out of here with Gagarin?"

The man nodded again.

"Excellent."

And turning to the professor, he said, "Untie the cuff and gag. I can't do it with my hand like this."

And then to the man, "Now, you're not going to give Gagarin another of those orders, right? Because if you did that, I'd have to hurt you both, a lot," he said, pointing to the machete. "And neither of us wants that."

The man shook his head several times.

"If you do that, I'll split your monkey's head in two."

More shakes of the head.

"Excellent. Whenever you're ready, come in here with me, please."

With that, and under the steady gaze of the elderly couple, Joanes retreated to the bathroom with the chimpanzee, which hobbled along behind him.

"What's going on?" asked the professor's wife.

"I don't know. I think the kid's lost it."

"And is that any surprise?"

The professor didn't answer. He untied the man as he'd been ordered to do and withdrew a few steps, putting himself in between his wife and the stranger, who got to his feet and looked around, disoriented. He massaged his wrists and felt his head.

"You ought to do what he says," said the professor.

The man nodded and followed Joanes, his back stooped.

The elderly couple kept their eyes on the entrance to the bathroom. The wind veiled whatever words were being spoken in the dark and almost in whispers inside.

"Did you say anything to the kid?" asked the professor.

"No."

"What were you two talking about?"

"We weren't talking about anything."

"Why did you let him take the machete?"

"What could I do?"

Soon after, Joanes left the bathroom, the chimpanzee still in tow. The elderly couple looked at him expectantly, but he simply walked past them in silence, not even catching their eye. He picked up the flashlight then went into the little room were the professor had gone earlier, and he closed the door.

Joanes switched on the flashlight and put it on the floor. He studied his maimed hand, the empty space where his now severed fingers had been. If he kept it still, he only felt a kind of faint, throbbing pain, as if his arm stretched out many, many feet ahead of him and he were looking at his hands through a telescope. If he tried to move it, it was a whole other story—the pain was lacerating, almost unbearable. The monkey had collapsed on the floor against a wall with his head down.

Not much time had passed when he heard a scream in the other room. The chimpanzee jumped, forcing Joanes to hold the cane firmly.

It was the professor's wife. The scream only stopped when the last drop of air had left her lungs. Straight afterward, through the sound of the wind, strangled voices and hard thumps could be heard. Then, for a moment, nothing, and the storm suddenly roared doubly loud.

He heard more blows. And then a noise like something falling to the ground. After this, a pause and then another scream, once again coming from the professor's wife.

Joanes left the cane on the floor; this forced him to relinquish control of the chimpanzee, but he had to take that risk. In any case, in its current state, the monkey didn't pose much of a threat. He clutched the machete firmly. The door boomed when someone knocked on it from the other side.

"Sir?" said the man, shouting to be heard over the wind.

"All done?" shouted Joanes.

His voice sounded exceptionally loud in the tiny space of the room.

"Yes, sir."

There was a pause, and then Joanes asked, "Sure?"

"Yes, sir."

"Now I want you to cover them up. Use the blankets on the bed."

Another pause.

"Is Gagarin all right?" the man wanted to know.

"Do what I tell you!"

A moment later the man was knocking again.

"I've done what you asked," he shouted.

"Now I want you to go into the bathroom, and I don't want you to move. Once you're inside, shout so I know you're there. Got it?"

"Yes, sir."

"If I see you when I open this door, I'll kill your monkey. Understood?"

"But you promised me that—"

"I don't give a shit what I promised you! I see you, I kill it."

A second later the man said, "OK!"

A few moments passed, and he heard the man calling that he was in the bathroom. His voice sounded far away. Joanes decided it was best to leave the monkey where it was. Then he picked up the flashlight from the floor and took a deep breath. But he still didn't leave. He stayed there unmoving, his hand on the door handle, allowing himself a few more seconds, making the most of the refuge afforded him by those four walls.

166

The door to the cabin was open and swinging in the wind. The night and the storm were blasting in. The bed had fallen apart. The mattress was lying on the dirty floor. The bricks that had supported the corner of the frame had fallen over. The bucket where they'd made the fire was tipped on its head, and the cinders were scattered all around. The wind made glowing threads appear in the embers and whipped up the trash.

Joanes moved toward the door. He found the woman lying with her legs on the inside of the cabin and the upper part of her body sprawled across the stoop. The professor was next to the car. The two bodies had each been carefully covered with several blankets. The wind was doing its best to carry away their shrouds. A brick lay in the mud, and the rain was washing away the blood on it.

As he looked down at the soaking lump that was the professor's body, Joanes didn't feel any relief. His only thought was that now he wouldn't have the chance to clear up their unfinished business. The disconcertion he felt at his own response would later transform into a kind of bitterness he'd have to consciously reflect on in order to properly define.

He called the man, who came out of the bathroom leaning against the wall for support. On seeing him, Joanes stifled a cry of surprise. The man's face was covered in scratches, as if he'd been attacked with a rake. One of the wounds cut across his eye. His torso was bare and his chest scored with more cuts.

"I've done everything you asked me to."

When the man spoke, Joanes caught a glimpse of his teeth, which were covered in blood.

"So the old man put up a fight," Joanes said.

"And her. She put up a fight, too. Will you give me Gagarin now? Can we go?"

"First close the door."

"You're going to leave those two out there, getting wet?"

"I don't think they mind."

The man closed and braced the door. In order to do so, he had to move the woman's body to one side.

"Where's Gagarin?"

"In the other room."

"Is he all right?"

"Perfectly fine."

"Can we go now?"

"Soon," said Joanes.

Then he added, "It's raining hard now."

"But—"

"Sit, please."

The man obeyed.

"Can I see my friend?"

"Don't worry about him," said Joanes, then he lit the oil lamp and turned off the flashlight.

"That's better," he said, taking a seat on the floor at a safe distance from the man. "What's your name?"

"Abraham."

"Do your friends call you Abe?"

168

"I don't have any friends."

"Your acquaintances, then?"

"Some."

"All right. I'll call you Abraham."

And then he added, "Abraham, we should be clear about what's just happened. You've just killed two people. You've taken their lives. Let's not forget that. And I'm telling you this is case you should have any intention of going to the police."

Abraham didn't say a word.

"If you told anyone I forced you to do it, nobody would believe you. And if it came to that, I could show them how you attacked me, which would make your story even harder to believe," said Joanes, holding up his maimed hand.

Now Abraham lowered his head and began to cry.

"Who were they?" he asked after a while.

"That doesn't matter. They weren't anybody to you. You don't need to know what they were called or who they were. It's enough for me to know. You, Abraham, are not really responsible for what happened tonight. You didn't have any choice but to act as you did, because you had to protect Gagarin. And you love him as if he were a son, isn't that right?"

Abraham nodded.

"He's the only friend I have."

"Of course he is, Abraham. You had to defend him. You did well. You fulfilled your duty."

And with that, Abraham burst into tears again. Joanes stretched out his legs in an effort to get comfortable. He was trying not to think about the pain in his hand and nose.

"Why not tell me a bit about yourself," he said, "while the storm blows over."

Abraham looked at him, uncomprehending, his eyes full of tears.

"I want to know all about you, Abraham."

"Why?"

"Because now, Abraham, you are someone very important to me."

And he repeated, "Very important."

A moment later, Abraham began to talk.

"Louder. I can't hear you."

Abraham began again.

Above them, the hurricane continued its northward course, transforming the thermal energy it had drained from the Caribbean Sea into kinetic energy, consuming itself in the process. It pressed on anxiously toward the Gulf of Mexico, into which it would flow hours later, gaining even more force, puffing up like a magnificent male in mating season.

The air was still unsettled in the morning. The clouds looked like they were resting on top of the trees. It was raining and windy, though not like the night before. At around noon, a jeep came by, careening down the track that led to the cabin. It stopped when it reached the building, and all four doors of the vehicle opened at once. The owner of the English Residence got out, escorted by three relatives, and looked at the place, frowning.

They couldn't see Joanes's car anywhere. The door to the cabin was wide open. They went in. Inside, the place was wet and covered in dead leaves and trash. They saw a bed frame with one leg missing, a soaking mattress, and the remains of a fire. In the middle of the main room, a load of boards were heaped one on top of another. When one of the relatives asked about them, the owner of the English Residence said that they used to shield the windows, and that some son of a bitch had ripped them off. The wind and rain had breezed in and swept the cabin clean.

The hotel owner said that nobody would spend the night in a place like that, least of all on a night like the one they'd just seen. His relatives agreed. They all took it as a given that the Spaniards, on seeing the state of the place, would have moved right on, looking for a better option.

Even so, the hotel owner was hesitant to leave without at least checking for signs that they'd been there. He inspected each and every one of the rooms but came across no more than some sodden trash. Before climbing back into the jeep, he took a second to study the vegetation around the cabin. He didn't see a thing, not a single clue, and he said a silent prayer in the hope that the man and those elderly folks were safe and well.

From where he was, in the middle of the thick vegetation, Joanes couldn't make out the sound of the jeep's motor. Now both his hands hurt, the maimed one and the other, which was riddled with splinters from where he'd wrenched the boards from the windows.

He was in a small clearing, leaning against a tree. His right hand was resting on the handle of the machete, which he was carrying in his belt. The chimpanzee was crouching on the ground at his side.

In the middle of the clearing, spurred by the threat that if he tried anything, the monkey would die, Abraham had just finished digging a grave. The earth oozed moisture—a black, fragrant mulch that kept slipping back into the hole. Abraham was covered in dirt, as if he'd been rolling around in the mud. On his face, only his eyes and teeth were visible. He worked on his knees, his sole tool being a dented aluminum plate that he'd selected from among his odds and ends and was using as a shovel.

They'd had to wait for sunrise before setting to work. By then, they'd already wrenched the boards from the windows. Earlier that morning, before doing anything else, they'd removed the dead bodies from sight, hiding them for the time being in the undergrowth.

The next step now was to move the car off the cabin track and stow it in some hidden corner on the road. Joanes had already guessed someone from the hotel would turn up in the morning. He put the woman's wheelchair in the trunk. He also stored the elderly couple's luggage and the things the owner of the English Residence had given them. He'd get rid of all that later on. Finally, he grabbed his own meager luggage.

He told Abraham to wait for him in the cabin. He didn't bother to tie him up, since the easiest way to stop him from running off was to keep ahold of the chimpanzee. And yet, driving and watching over the monkey at the same time would have been too tricky, and in any case the chimpanzee would have been too conspicuous if they'd come across anyone on the road. Once the cabin was out of sight, he tied the monkey's chain to a tree and left him there.

When he came back a while later, he had a little scare. The chimpanzee wasn't moving. It was resting against the tree trunk with its head slumped to one side. Joanes thought it was dead. If that was the case, he would have no way of controlling Abraham. He nudged the chimpanzee with one end of the cane.

"Come on, Gagarin. Don't fail me now."

He nudged him again.

The chimpanzee slowly stirred. The hood covering his head moved from one side to another. Joanes let out a big sigh of relief.

When he was just a couple of paces from the cabin, Joanes stopped and called to Abraham. He ordered him to come out with his hands above his head.

"You're not going to give me any surprises, are you, Abraham?"

Abraham shook his head.

"That's what I like to hear. Now walk here in front of me. Not too fast. Not too slow."

Together they went in search of an appropriate place to bury the professor and his wife. The monkey followed them, attached to Joanes by the chain and cane, tripping over the roots of the trees.

Abraham stopped several times as he dug the grave, encumbered by great sobbing attacks. Once or twice he vomited a few gloopy threads of bile. He told Joanes that he couldn't get the faces of the professor and his wife the moment they died out of his head, that he'd never forget them, and Joanes responded by saying that that was exactly what he had to do. He, Abraham, from then on, was a container for the memory of the last moments of those elderly people's lives. Abraham was silent for a few seconds and then began to mumble about something the professor had done before dying. Joanes pointed the machete at him and ordered him to be quiet.

"It's enough for you to know and remember what happened," he added.

When the time came to lower the bodies down, Abraham got out of the hole and took a few steps back. Pushing them with one foot, Joanes rolled the professor and his wife into the grave. He enjoyed the slight resistance their bodies gave. He'd stripped them of their wallets, watches, and wedding rings beforehand. She wasn't wearing any other jewelry. He told Abraham to cover them up.

The pain in his hand observed a cruel, arcane logic. It came and went in waves. At its most intense, Joanes felt like he needed to run, to do anything that might distract him from the pain. Instead, he vented some of it by ordering Abraham to work faster. Abraham looked at him, his eyes red from exhaustion, tears, and the earth that had gotten in them, but barely changing his pace.

Despite the pain and tiredness, Joanes felt tremendously lucid. The night before, he'd had time to plan what he had to do. As soon as they got rid of the bodies, he'd look for a doctor to fix him up and give him a rabies shot. He'd explain the injuries by saying that a vagrant dog had attacked him. He'd gotten lost looking for the evacuation hotel and hadn't had any choice but to spend the night in his car. When he'd set off the following morning, he'd gone over a broken branch and gotten a flat tire. While he was changing it, the dog had attacked him, or rather several dogs, a pack. That's what he'd tell whoever asked him. A simple, perfectly believable story, something that could easily happen to a careless tourist who didn't know the area and didn't have any experience with hurricanes. Then he'd go to Valladolid, back to his family.

On the off chance that anyone should ask him about the professor and his wife, he'd admit that he'd picked them up on the highway, and also that they'd stopped briefly at the English Residence, where they'd been asked to leave. On seeing the uninhabitable state of the cabin, they'd all decided to move on, until, totally lost, they'd had to stop. He would confirm that the last time he'd seen them was that same morning, when he left them safe and sound at the bus station in a nearby town.

But he was pretty sure that nobody was going to probe his story further. He supposed there'd be other lost tourists, accidents, and that the hurricane would have left several victims in its wake, far more important things than someone having been attacked by a bunch of dogs. And he supposed that nobody ever set foot in that clearing. And he also supposed that the avid tropical soil would soon dissolve the bodies. All of these, to him, were completely plausible suppositions.

"It's done," said Abraham.

"Get up. Go over there by that tree and don't move."

Joanes looked over the place.

"You've done a nice job, Abraham."

"Can we go now?"

"That's what I promised you. But this," said Joanes, gesturing at the machete, "and this," pointing to the cane on the ground, "are staying with me. You can take your monkey."

Abraham got down on his knees next to Gagarin and with trembling hands unleashed him from the tree to which he'd been chained. He took off the makeshift handcuffs behind his back and, finally, removed the hood. The monkey blinked and looked from one side to the other. He let out a long moan. There were dry, bloody scabs on his head and on one of his ears, which had been bleeding from the inside.

"Gagarin, Gagarin . . ." repeated his master, who burst into tears again. "My friend."

The chimpanzee leaned in toward him, and the two embraced. They stayed there like that for a long time, under the attentive eye of Joanes, who eventually said, "I'll give you some cash. You can hold on to the flashlight, too; I'm sure it'll come in handy. Although you'll have to come to the car with me to find it."

Abraham didn't answer. He was stroking Gagarin's back.

"If I can do anything else to help you . . ."

At last, Abraham got to his feet. The only response he gave Joanes was a look of absolute and intense contempt.

Then, swinging his backpack over his shoulder, he picked Gagarin up in his arms. The chimpanzee rested his head on his master's shoulder and closed his eyes.

"Goodbye, Abraham. Look after yourself."

Joanes watched as Abraham and the monkey walked off into the distance, gradually blending into the vegetation, and eventually disappearing altogether. Not long after, he thought he heard a sort of song, a lullaby, but he couldn't be sure. All around him was the *drip-drip* of raindrops falling from every leaf of every tree.

Hours later, once Joanes had erased all trace of himself as best he could and scattered a few branches over the stirred up soil, and once he'd given the place a last once-over and left for the car, leaving the clearing that had now returned to its normal calm, a magnificent specimen of a boa constrictor appeared there. It was an adult female, over six feet long, and it was looking for any baby chicks that had been pitched from their nests by the storm. It stopped in the middle of the clearing, lifted up its head, stuck out its black tongue, and writhed its body until it was half buried, as if it were trying to take a mud bath. Then it slithered toward a nearby tree, which it proceeded to scale. The track left in the mud by its powerful body looked like a sort of strange, sinuous signature. Curled up on a branch that stuck out over the clearing, it waited.

In the end, after several hours spent trying to fall asleep, Joanes got out of bed. His wife groaned and changed position. He opened the sliding door that led out onto the balcony and went outside for some air. It was a pleasant spring night. The window of the next-door room was lit up. His daughter must still be awake, probably still working away on her never-ending, nihilistic vampire novel. The manuscript consisted of a bundle of three thick notebooks tied together with elastic bands. Up to this point, she still hadn't let her parents read any of it.

He considered knocking on her door and telling her to go to sleep, but he couldn't face an argument at that hour. His daughter seemed stranger and stranger to him, even though Joanes also accepted that this was normal, if perhaps it had happened a little sooner than he'd expected it to. He would later tell himself that this was also normal.

He looked at his wife through the sliding door. She'd pulled off the sheets in her sleep. He couldn't see her face, which was buried in the pillow. Looking in from there, under the orangey light of the streetlamps, the room looked different—bigger and more inviting. He felt the guilty pang of a voyeur.

A short while after, the light in his daughter's room went off. Joanes looked out at the street, which was lined with trees and stone-façaded houses. A few days earlier, he and his wife had given up on the idea of moving to a bigger place, a dream they'd been harboring for years. Better to forget about that till things were going better. At first it had really saddened Joanes, but now he didn't care.

He took a deep breath, filling his lungs with air that was itself full of the promise of summer. He felt good. If some messenger from the future had appeared before him and announced that from there on out, things would neither get any better nor any worse for him than they were right then at that moment, he wouldn't have had too much trouble getting used to the idea.

ABOUT THE AUTHOR

JON BILBAO is a Spanish literary writer, translator and scriptwriter who lives in Bilbao. He has published the novels *El hermano de las moscas, Padres, hijos y primates* (*Still the Same Man*) and *Shakespeare y la ballena blanca*, as well as the short story collections *Como una historia de terror* and *Bajo el influjo del cometa*. He has won the Premio Asturias Joven de Narrativa, the Premio Ojo Crítico de Narrativa, the Premio Tigre Juan and the Premio Euskadi de Narrativa.

ABOUT THE TRANSLATOR

SOPHIE HUGHES' translations have appeared in *Asymptote Journal, Words Without Borders, PEN Atlas*, the *Guardian* and *The White Review*. She has also written for the *Times Literary Supplement, Dazed & Confused, Music & Literature* and the *Literary Review*. In 2015 she was awarded the British Centre for Literary Translation prose mentorship. She has also translated novels by Iván Repila, Laia Jufresa, and Rodrigo Hasbún.

Lightning Source UK Ltd.
Milton Keynes UK
UKOW04f1424140216

268285UK00001B/1/P